Introducing the first Scandalous Bride…

"How fortunate a man I am to have such a beauty eager for me ruin her," Crawford murmured.

Amity placed her hands on his chest again, feeling the heat of him seep through to warm her gloved fingers. "Very eager to get it done, and quickly."

"A proper seduction should not be rushed, but given the danger of marriage, a rush is what you'll get." He bent close and nuzzled her cheek with his lips. "Are you ready?"

Wicked with Him

Heather Boyd

The characters and events portrayed in this book are fictitious. Any similarity to real persons, living or dead, is purely coincidental and not intended by the author.

Editing by Kelli Collins

Chapter One

Roman Crawford felt a tug on the back of his coat and turned his attention from the ballroom to see who had snuck up behind him unannounced.

"Don't turn to look at me," a woman whispered urgently.

He tried not to roll his eyes. Past lovers could be so tedious sometimes when they hoped to regain his attention. But he didn't recognize this particular woman's voice, so no doubt it was a lady long forgotten and of the belief that he would enliven her evening if offered a chance to get under her skirts again. She was in for a rude realization. He had loved and lost, and had no time for any game but his own. "Why shouldn't I look? Clearly you seek my attention."

"I don't want my family seeing me talking to you," the woman whispered with fear in her voice.

In Roman's experience, neglected women tended to *want* people to look at them and become jealous, to prove they still mattered. He scanned the ballroom for familiar faces, for husbands of previous lovers, but saw none within his immediate view.

He relaxed but truly wanted to turn and end the game, though he had to admit he was amused by her stealthy approach. "Who would your family be?"

There was a long pause. "You don't recognize me by my voice?"

He shook his head. The voice nagged his memory but not enough to produce a name to match its sweet tones. "No."

"I feared as much." The woman sighed heavily. "We've never spoken directly to each other, sir."

He almost laughed out loud. "Then how could I know your family?"

"You do know some of *them* well, but you are not on good terms with my side. Not that I blame you."

"You have my complete attention now," he murmured, straightening and letting his eyes sweep the room one more time. There were many in this room whom he knew well indeed, depending on the length of their acquaintance. There were few he actively loathed though.

One irritating creature stood directly across from him, holding court among his cronies. His senses came alert when he noticed an absence in that man's vicinity.

"For how long has this dislike been so apparent?"

"At least the last year," she said quietly.

He stiffened as the only possibility immediately came to mind. The softly spoken woman behind him could only be a connection of the despicable creature he was trying to ruin. George Sweet had been a target of Roman's rage for one year exactly. Everyone knew why. "And would you happen to be a *close* relative?"

"Unfortunately, yes."

He turned his head slightly. "Sweet Paragon?"

"Shh," the woman hissed, confirming his guess about her identity was correct.

Roman knew exactly who was trying to talk to him, and why she was trying so hard not to be seen. He could hardly believe she'd dare. Lady Amity Sweet, niece to the current Duke of Ravenswood, sister to the man he loathed beyond all reason, shouldn't have sought him out. Not unless she was wanted to be used in Roman's bid for unending revenge against her older brother. She could be ruined in the blink of an eye. "How may I be of assistance?"

"Ruin me."

Roman blinked, believing he'd misheard his own thought coming from her lips. "I beg your pardon?"

"Ten minutes. Beneath the staircase. Meet me there and tell no one."

No one would believe him if he did, anyway. He could hardly believe he was the recipient of such a scandalous invitation from her of all people.

Roman glanced over his shoulder into the darkness and found Lady Amity Sweet, slender and lovely to behold, huddled against the outer wall of the townhouse. "Now why would I want to risk my neck sneaking off with you when I could ruin you here just as well as anywhere," he snarled. "If I ever wanted to."

She straightened from the wall. "Because being found together does not suit either of our purposes," she snapped. "You're used to ladies you barely know making requests for you to meet them for a tryst. You never see them again. One more scandalous liaison could hardly be a burden now, could it?"

He was surprised Lady Amity had noticed the way he treated the women in his life—or dared mention them to his face. Women were temporary amusements unless it's the one you loved.

Yes, many women sought him out for an all-too-brief fling. But Lady Amity Sweet *never* should. The woman was an incomparable. A diamond of the first water. Followed and guarded day and night. Had she had enough of her status at the top of the heap and slipped away for a taste of danger?

He glanced around again, weighing up the significance of her approach. If Amity wouldn't guard her reputation from scandal, why the hell should he worry about it?

Roman had already considered what use Amity might be to him, but there was only so far he would go extracting his revenge, of course. He did not ruin innocents.

Not like her brother had.

But Amity was well placed to feed him information about her brother's interests in the future. He was already well advanced on a way to impact George Sweet's pocket this week. There was no way to immediately benefit from the woman's approach, aside from the ruin she asked for.

He would send her on her way for now but perhaps arrange to meet at a later time.

Ever since George Sweet had ruined and married the love of Roman's life, he had gone out of his way to interfere in George's private affairs. Roman had spent the last year actively working toward spoiling her brother's chances of success every time their interests collided. They were enemies. They moved in the same circles thanks to his money, but otherwise ignored each other in public.

And Amity had now come to him for ruin.

He stepped into the dark with her, keen to hear her reasons and to arrange a further meeting far from prying eyes. "Be quick in explaining or you'll be ruined just standing here alone with me."

"But that is what I want. Ruin, and tonight."

She couldn't be serious. He stalked toward her. "Say that again."

Her hands landed on his chest to hold him back from crowding her too closely. "I know what he did to you and Melody, and I hate him for separating you from the woman you loved. I could do nothing then. Now I need your help to stop him meddling in *my* love life."

Of course, Amity should have suitors by the dozens…but the mention of them irked him. She was beautiful and well-dowered and connected to a powerful family. But her brother, and the rest of her family, had kept any circling fortune hunters at bay up until now. "Whom do you love and not wish to be separated from?"

"That is none of your concern." Her fingertips scraped his chest as she balled her hand into a fist. "My family have arranged for a proposal of marriage to be made to me tonight without my agreement or encouragement. Before everyone. I will not be a pawn, married off against my will, but they will not listen to me. Not with the Duke of Ravenswood giving his blessing to the union, too."

Ravenswood, Amity's uncle, was an influential figure in society, of course. His sons were acquaintances of Roman's, and more to his taste since they disliked their cousin George almost as much as Roman did. While annoying George Sweet was always a pleasure, infuriating four strapping lords and a duke was not his goal.

"I take it you want them to regret underestimating you by any means available," Roman drawled.

"Yes," she insisted.

"I still don't see how ruining you is anything but a punishment for me. I don't want to marry you, I'm afraid."

"I don't want to marry you, either," she shot back in a hiss of sound that impressed him for its venom. "I only want your help to make it clear I've been ravished...before any proposal of marriage can be uttered. When it's clear I'm not the paragon they boast about, their choice for my husband will rethink his decision and perhaps they'll give me peace."

He inhaled sharply, believing her. But caution was called for. "This is certainly a trap."

"Only for them, I swear. They're so pleased with the match, and convinced I'll just go meekly into this man's bed, that they can't conceive I'd try to thwart them. But I will have my freedom, one way or another. *Your* revenge will be taken in secret as you view George's public humiliation."

"Embarrassing for you, too, Sweet Paragon," he warned, dragging his fingertips up her arms. "Especially when I will not come forward to say it was me who lifted your skirts."

"I'll hold you to the promise not to speak up and claim my ridiculously high dowry for yourself," she whispered, drawing her hands slowly down his chest until she was no longer touching him. "Society is about to find out just how badly their description suits me. It's beyond the pale that his grace started the rumor that gave me the title Sweet Paragon before I came out, and now no sensible man dares think themselves good enough to come courting without gaining his approval first."

"Ravenswood started the rumors about your purity himself?"

"I remember the night with perfect clarity. All the family were present. My wiser male cousins all but fell off their chairs laughing at the description. More interesting men have been avoiding me ever since I came out because of a stupid name."

Amity had been on the marriage mart for some years now. Most of those who'd come out the same year were long married, and a lot had already given their husbands their heirs. "I merely thought you were overly particular," he murmured.

"My *family* is. But how would you know fact from fiction when we've never spoken before, and why would you have when it was clear you were besotted by your Melody?"

He had been, and had been taunted for missing out on her dowry ever since, too. But that was not why he'd pursued Melody to marry him. He was in love with the sweet, innocent girl, tricked into a similar situation that now faced Amity.

Amity tugged on his sleeve. "Will you ruin me?"

He lifted his hand and brushed hers off his arm. "I'm ruining you now."

"You think me naïve? I am well aware of the

requirements for a tryst. This is a bad location for one. You need to get away cleanly and there are only two exits here, and both lead to the revel makers inside."

He'd rather not be found with his breeches down around his ankles and Amity's pale legs wrapped about his waist. He cast his eyes about the balcony and saw that she had a point, there were no other exits unless he wanted to risk breaking his neck in a fall. "I take it you've been planning the matter of your ruin quite seriously?"

"I've seen enough scandals and forced marriages to know location is vital to avoid detection. A balcony will be the first place my brother will search for me."

He grunted. "Where were you to offer advice on the night your brother stole Melody away from me," he grumbled.

"In the ballroom, along with everyone else watching events unfold. A terrace is where they slipped away to. Five minutes. Meet me," she urged, and then she glided back into the ballroom, chin high as ever, serene smile gracing her lips.

Roman shook his head before returning to his spot holding up the doorframe, pretending nothing had happened as he watched the dancers pass him by.

No one seemed to have missed him, but he noticed Amity's brother was looking around rather anxiously. Roman held his breath. He spotted Amity talking with a male cousin, and George

Sweet visibly relaxed too, before he turned back to his circle of friends with a laugh.

The supercilious jackass was so in love with his own importance, Roman felt sick to his stomach that another woman was at his mercy.

He wasn't truly surprised George would try to control his lovely sister by forcing her into a marriage she didn't desire, too. It would serve him right to have his night befouled by a scandal, though he could hardly believe Amity would be serious about the matter—or that he was considering agreeing to her request. Surely, she could have chosen someone else to ruin her tonight. Someone better suited to marriage should they be found together would be best.

However, as he studied the fellows loitering in the ballroom, he easily saw why she'd approached him, of all people. She was desperate, and this room was filled with the most ambitious, scheming younger sons in society—all with their eye on marrying well to increase their own fortunes. A collection of entitled prigs with empty pockets watched her closely even now. Roman might be the only bachelor present who did not need money nor want to marry someone with a large dowry

He glanced at his pocket watch. Five minutes till Amity's planned rendezvous. Should he meet with her under the stairs? It certainly was tempting, even without her assurances. *She* tempted him…and it might have nothing at all to do with revenge.

He wasn't blind. Amity was a stunning woman, and the thought of her with someone else for her first time sat ill with him.

It was just an added bonus that if he played along with her scheme, he'd see George Sweet brought low by scandal all in one evening.

And if he didn't end up trapped in a marriage with Amity, he should have no regrets or suffer guilt. Amity clearly had everything figured out. Location to meet before heading off, timing, his escape route, and her eventual discovery alone, no doubt. She was against her brother, which made her a friend of Roman's forever.

But did he dare take the risk he wasn't being played for a fool? He was curious how far she'd go. A kiss? Far more? A proper ruin? That was what she claimed to want from him.

He'd only find out the truth if he met with her.

Roman moved from his spot, circling the room so he would pass close to George Sweet before he decided. The man laughed like a braying ass, his wife—Roman's sweet Melody, by his side forever now instead of Roman's—was smiling up at her husband as if she'd only ever loved him.

Roman gritted his teeth and continued out of the ballroom, turning toward the staircase and then passing under. He saw no guest or servant who might remember he'd walked this way. But there was also no sign of Amity either, which disappointed him thoroughly.

He paused behind the stairs, believing he'd been led a merry dance. "Damn the whole lot of them."

A creak reached his ears then a woman's hand shot out of the shadows of a hidden door, gripped his arm, and hauled him into a tiny chamber under the very staircase. He had visited this house many times and never noticed its existence.

Chapter Two

Amity peered up at the man bent over her. "What kept you?"

There was a long pause. "I'm here, my sweet," Crawford drawled finally, relieving her no end that she'd grabbed the right man in her hurry to drag him inside. She had feared Roman Crawford would let her down. He'd not really seemed keen to help her with her plan to ruin herself, and she didn't blame him for mistrusting her motives, given what her brother had done to him in the past.

Amity wished she might see her would-be lover but would make do. She was about to be ruined. "Do not ever make more jests with my name," she hissed.

He chuckled softly, his breath stirring the tendrils of her hair about her ear. "I cannot help myself. Has there ever been a more poorly chosen name for such a devious a woman?"

Amity shivered. "Devious in thought only until tonight, unlike my cousins, who practice the art of debauchery in your company on every possible occasion," she said bitterly, thinking of the lengths she'd been driven to by her older brother's ambitions and her families' machinations. She'd learned to hate her name and the association of purity that was attached to her skin. She had been made into the reluctant paragon of the family, her virtue considered a priceless commodity to be traded for wealth and connections by her older brother and her uncle the duke.

Well, no longer would she be their pawn. Tonight, she'd be ruined well and truly with Roman Crawford's help.

"Your cousin, and his brothers, are men more to my taste," he promised. "The rest can go to hell."

"I agree, and my brother first of all," she murmured, feeling fury build inside her again as it had done for weeks now. Her brother thought he'd the right to trade her like cattle by marrying her off to the highest bidder. Well, she'd not let that happen. She'd rather engineer her own ruin than accept a husband her family chose.

She did not approve of marrying a pork-bellied buffoon who already wouldn't let her speak her mind.

She took a steadying breath to release her temper. Roman Crawford loomed over her in the dark, making her feel small and decidedly breathless, she found. His normally sleepy honey-brown eyes were hidden in the dark, but she knew his fondness for mischief with other ladies and for causing chaos when it came to her brother's interests. She was grateful he jumped at the chance to accommodate her suggestion to meet in private.

His hands settled lightly about her upper arms. "Definitely your brother first. Then, after tonight, let's hope he suffers apoplexy from the shock of how he'll find you and dies."

"As long as he doesn't find me with you, I'll be satisfied that he lives forever disappointed in me. But I must warn you, George wouldn't hesitate to call you out and shoot you dead tomorrow morning. I insist you disappear as soon as we're done."

Roman's fingers, now bare of gloves, traced a pattern up and down her arm. "I admit, I'm not keen to die by his sword or pistol at dawn…or do you think me unequal to such a challenge?"

"Not at all. I should only rather you did not have to kill him and flee the country after. That would be grossly unfair after all you've suffered at his hands. He would certainly try to kill you, I'm sure, and not just because of me. You're causing him no end of trouble."

"Because of Melody."

"I am truly sorry about her," she whispered, laying her hands on his chest. "And I promise you won't be sorry about *me*."

It was no secret Crawford had set his cap for her now sister-in-law two years ago. Courting her with sweet poetry and constant attention. Amity had heard some. George had read aloud Roman's beautiful love letters one night to everyone in the household to hear. But Crawford had not been the only man circling Melody, and the vain, foolish woman had played right into George's hands and ended up married to him instead someone better.

Just because George wanted it that way, wanted her dowry, not because of a deeper bond of affection for the woman. The pair were *not* happily married. In public, they of course pretended to be happy with the match, but in private, at home, the chill and fury between them was unbearable.

Ever since that dreadful marriage, Crawford had subtly interfered in just about every aspect of her brother's life. He'd lured away their chef, and her brother's valet, too. Purchased livestock intended for their country estate but not already paid for. He'd been quite inventive really, exacting any number of small revenges. Amity had found her brother's frustration of late quite satisfying to watch. But she'd known deep down that Crawford wasn't done with her brother. That helped with her situation.

"How fortunate a man I am to have such a beauty eager for me ruin her."

She placed her hands on his chest again, feeling the heat of him seep through to warm her gloved fingers. "Very eager to get it done, and quickly."

"A proper seduction should not be rushed, but given the danger of marriage, a rush is what you'll get." He bent close and nuzzled her cheek with his lips. "Are you ready?"

"Indeed. I know my brother won't allow me out of his sight for long."

"Hopefully he'll not come before you do." His fingers suddenly swept across the top of her breasts, and she jumped at the contact. "I've always believed a woman should enjoy her deflowering."

"I suppose that depends on your skill," she murmured.

"I love a challenge."

Crawford was reputed to be very experienced with women interested in short-term affairs. That was why she'd chosen him out of all others she could have picked. She believed he wouldn't offer marriage to claim her dowry, although if he did, that would *really* infuriate her brother.

Crawford suddenly tilted her chin up and pressed a kiss to her lips.

Unused to such things, Amity's first thought was to push him back. But her resistance lasted only a moment as she remembered why she was alone with Crawford in the first place. She had a job to see done.

She received his next kisses with more enthusiasm. His hands slid restlessly all over her body, attempting to excite her no doubt, but she wasn't sure what to do with her own fingers. Crawford must have sensed her confusion, because he slid his hands down her arms, caught her wrists, and slowly raised them to drape over his shoulders, nudging them higher until she embraced him, all the while kissing her with increasing passion.

They swayed like that in the dark for several long minutes. Crawford explored her curves while she held him, overwhelmed by the new experiences.

He drew back. "You're a lovely woman, but part your lips for me," he demanded impatiently.

As soon as she did, he teased his tongue into her mouth—and the wonders of kissing became all too apparent. She grew hot as his hands rose again, sliding firmly up her back until he held her tightly against him at her shoulders, and intensified the kisses he delivered with such stunning passion.

Amity moaned softly. She had known some of what to expect but *nothing* had prepared her for the onslaught of desire Crawford stirred in her. She could barely get enough of his kisses now.

When Crawford lifted her skirt and caught hold of her bare thigh, she eased her body against his without shame or hesitation.

He drew back and nibbled on her ear, sending shivers racing down her spine, and then whispered, "Do you ache between your legs yet, sweetheart?"

"Hmm, yes, I believe so. Is that important?"

"Essential," he whispered. "You'll enjoy this even more."

He urged her backward against the wall and brushed his hips against her lower body. Although the fabric of her skirts and his breeches lay between them, her ache became so much more urgent after that. For the first time in her adult life, she embraced the danger of wrinkling her own gown for the benefit of more pleasure.

It felt so good to be wicked with him.

Crawford eased her skirts to her waist. His bare fingers were rough and hot against her thighs and hips. She felt a cool draft swirl around her lower half…and then his hand was pressing firmly over her sex.

Amity bucked from the shockingly intimate sensation.

"Easy," he whispered. "The first caress here is bound to be a surprise."

"Everything about you is a surprise so far," she whispered back, gulping down her shock.

"Wait till you feel me inside you," he whispered. "Then it feels strangest of all but in a good way, I swear."

She could not help but laugh at that. "Boastful."

"That's why you came to me, sweetheart. You needed a man of experience for this sort of adventure. Don't think about what we're doing or what happens next. Let your body follow mine."

"All right," she agreed, nodding quickly even though he couldn't possibly see her.

Amity closed her eyes and let him have his

way. This was what she'd come to him for anyway. She leaned into his touch, tilting her hips toward him when the urge struck or he encouraged her. Occasionally she had to turn her face away when the sensations of arousal became too shocking and made her breath catch.

Her eyes flew open, though, when he pressed inside her with his finger. Dear God! Now that wasn't something anyone had warned her a man might want to do. He thrust in and out a few times, slowly, and then withdrew to kiss her again.

She learned from Roman Crawford to thoroughly enjoy her ruin. The brush and slight burn of his stubble when he kissed her lips made her restless and decidedly hot. She tilted her hips toward him even more as the tension in her body rose to incredible heights.

When he stopped suddenly and exhaled, she whimpered in frustration. She wanted more of him.

Crawford chucked. "Best not forget what I'm here for."

"Oh, of course, yes," she said, and then swallowed. Being ruined seemed a much more enjoyable and prolonged business than she'd first assumed it might be.

She heard the unmistakable sound of him unbuttoning his trousers and the rustle of fabric as he must have pushed his clothes aside.

Amity gulped, but he gave her no time to consider a delay.

Instead, he lifted her up against the wall, wrapped her legs around his hips and pressed inside her.

At first, it was pleasant but then she hissed at the sting as he continued pushing into her.

"Breathe, lovely one," he whispered into her ear. "I won't hurt you more than I must."

Amity tried her best, but it felt too odd, too intimate to have him inside her. She strained up, ready to dislodge him completely.

Crawford grabbed her hands at the wrists and held them above her head against the wall. "We're not done yet, my lady. You wanted ruin, and by God you will have it done properly."

He drew back his hips and pressed back into her, again and again.

Amity turned her face aside, grateful that the dark hid her flaming cheeks from his sight.

His grip on her wrists softened, and then he gently wound her arms around his neck again. When he held her close, she could almost imagine there was tenderness between them in that small, dark space.

And she responded to that more than anything. What had initially caused pain now brought pleasure with every movement of his body inside hers. The ache between her legs slowly returned, only stronger somehow.

Crawford stroked her cheek softly. "Yes, now you feel it. Now you begin to understand the delights that await you."

She blushed even harder. She couldn't see him, but she felt him branded everywhere on her skin. She feared she might never forget Roman Crawford after this scandalous adventure.

Amity pressed her face into the crook of his neck, and Crawford cuddled her closer. They rocked together like that for some time. It was lovely. She had to admit, her lover seemed to know exactly what he was doing.

Crawford slipped a hand down onto her belly. "I need you to come."

"What?"

He chuckled against her ear. "You'll love it," he promised. "Widen your legs a bit more so my hand can fit between us."

When she did, Crawford leaned back a bit and slid his fingers into the space they'd created. He brushed across her sex and then teased his fingertips down lower, around his own cock inside her. When he slid those same fingers, now slippery wet, higher up, touching a spot so exquisitely sensitive, she moaned out loud and shuddered.

"Yes, sweetheart. I want you to feel passion tonight, too…but not too loud, if you don't mind. Whisper to me what you like."

Amity had assumed Crawford would do the deed and quickly vanish into the night. Not want to talk about it during the act of lovemaking and take his time pleasing her. "I like this."

"What exactly about this excites you?" he

asked, kissing her cheek while strumming over that sensitive spot again and again.

"*This*."

"Not my cock inside you?"

"Yes. No. All of it." She chuckled and looked up into his face. "*You*."

"Damn," he growled.

He suddenly started moving with more frenzy against her, inside her, his fingers pressing over that spot so sensitive and throbbing.

She immediately missed the slow tenderness of their beginning. The touches and caresses had made her ruin somehow less sordid and shameful.

His pace slowed again, and then he pressed hard into her body, but his touch became frenzied upon her sex. "Such a lovely tight cunny. So warm around me!"

Amity blushed and buried her face in his shoulder again. It shouldn't…but his compliment excited her. Aroused her even more.

"I never imagined I could have you, but I'm sure I'll never forget." Crawford suddenly eased her back against the wall. They were still joined at the hip as he grasped her bodice and jerked it down, ripping the fabric, and his hand settled on her bare breast. "I wish I could see you naked. My cock surging into you. Your breast tumbling out of your gown and my hand on these perfect plump orbs. Legs spread and my fingers teasing your clit to bring you to completion. My teeth grazing your lovely white shoulder. Giving you a lover's mark."

To illustrate his words, he bit down on her shoulder and lingered there a long time, sucking on her skin.

Amity shivered, holding him closer than ever. "Is that enough?"

"No," he huffed. He swore under his breath. "You're one of those women."

"What women?"

"The slow-to-find-completion type."

She frowned. "Is that bad?"

Crawford juggled her in his arms, holding her up entirely without the wall's help again. "Given tonight's urgency, it could be."

"I'm sorry," she whispered.

"Don't ever apologize for challenging me," he ordered. "I have never left a lady unsatisfied, and I'm not about to with you, either. Hold tight to me and don't let go."

This time when he touched her sex, she felt desire more powerfully, somehow. Crawford held her close, his hand persisting to tease her as he ground into her. They stood entwined in each other's arms, panting heavily as time seemed to stand still. They could have been the only two souls in the world. Except for the ballroom full of society's finest, her family standing among them.

Amity loved the slower pace better than everything he'd done to her so far that night. She tightened her legs around his hips to keep him as close as possible. She knew she must look utterly shameful with her legs wrapped around a near stranger, but she didn't care.

The sensations only grew in strength the longer they made love, until she couldn't think of anything else but reaching for more of that elusive sensation. Crawford grabbed her bare bum and rocked quickly against her.

Amity's back arched, and she dug her fingers into his shoulders, caught off guard by a sudden increase of feeling. Her body tightened all over and she whimpered, quickly trying to muzzle the sound of her cries.

"My God!" Crawford groaned.

And then it was over.

Crawford set her on her feet and drew back.

Amity's legs nearly buckled, and she put her hand out to the wall for support as she adjusted to the sudden end of Crawford's embrace. It took her a moment to get her bearings, but eventually she pushed her skirts down.

She also hurried to push her breasts back into her torn bodice and looked up at the dark shape before her. "Well…that's done and everything squared away."

Crawford said nothing to that.

"Well," she repeated, uncertain of how to go on with Crawford so quiet now. "You'd best be on your way, sir. Thank you."

He was suddenly clutching her elbow. "Should I stay?"

"No!" she cried and hurried to push him toward the secret door. The last thing she wanted was for him to develop a conscience. "You must go. My brother will be looking for me. You must go back to the ballroom. I'll go the long way round."

Crawford lingered. "Have you a plan for tomorrow, too? What if he throws you out tonight?"

"I should be so lucky. But he wouldn't dare. I'll be all right, I promise."

Crawford grunted.

She eased the door open, peeking out at the brighter light of the hallway, and although he seemed reluctant to leave her, Crawford stalked away unseen by anyone as far as she could tell.

Amity closed the door again and took a deep breath. Her next steps were crucial. She had to act as if nothing was wrong, all the while looking like she'd been ravished. She clung to the shadows of that secret room a little longer, mainly to give Roman more time to return to the ballroom by his route before she stepped out and took her chosen path. She stayed there as long as she dared, then she stepped out boldly to walk the halls, a proud and decidedly smug ruined lady.

Amity went to the retiring room first, intending to muss her hair more if it was needed and assess the damage done to her bodice. She hoped it was torn in an obvious place for any casual observer to notice.

As luck would have it, her sister-in-law was already there with a maid, primping before the mirror. Melody glanced up, smiling—and then her expression froze. "Sister?"

Melody only called her that when she was at her most condescending. Amity had never warmed to Melody. She'd learned quickly that any secret she told her brother's new wife would soon be whispered in his ear or to another member of the family out of spite. "Mrs. Sweet."

Amity moved toward a mirror to admire her appearance, tugging at her bodice to discover the location of the tear. Fixable, perhaps, but it would need a skilled hand, and for Amity to completely disrobe first. Her hair was falling from their pins, too, her lips pinkened and swollen from her skilled lover's kisses. She looked ruined—and that made her so very happy.

Melody met her gaze in the mirror, her mouth pinched with disapproval. Then she whirled about and fled the room.

Amity hummed a happy tune as she re-pinned parts of her hair very poorly in the mirror. She made no serious attempt to hide her ravishment, though. That was the point of being ruined tonight. Any moment, another member of the family would arrive, and then perhaps George as well to call her out as *scandalous*.

Amity grinned at her reflection in the mirror, enlightened, and happy as never before.

She put her fingers to her shoulder and traced

an angry red mark that suggested she'd been with a man intimately. She giggled, delighted with that, too. Roman Crawford had exceeded her expectations for their tryst. She hoped he had enjoyed having her, and that his view of her brother's rage and embarrassment was unimpeded when the time came to see it.

Deciding that enough time had passed for Melody to do her whispering, Amity waltzed out the door into the hall.

George was waiting. His face was set with fury. "Who did this to you?"

Amity smiled into her brother's angry eyes, and then glanced past him to a small crowd that hovered close behind—including the contender for her hand, his mouth agape in shock. Judging by everyone's stunned expressions, it was clearly obvious what had happened to her without having to say a single word.

There would be a scandal, she was ruined, and she'd at last stood up to her family.

Chapter Three

"Here," Lord Cushing whispered, pushing a piece of paper at Roman. "I believe this is what you were seeking more of."

Roman glanced at the details of a promissory note for fifty pounds and nodded. George Sweet seemed to owe everyone lately. Getting payment out of him appeared to be quite difficult for many of his acquaintances, though. This one was merely a small debt compared to some, but the value of those other notes Roman held in his safe was always increasing. From his pocket, he produced a wad of notes, slightly more than the value of the debt itself, and slipped it discreetly to Cushing's waiting hand. "Thank you."

"No, thank you," Cushing gushed and glided away again.

Cushing had been part of George Sweets' inner circle until recently. The loyalty of quite a few of his friends seemed to be unravelling of late. Greed and a wish to be made whole again won out more often than not.

Roman remained on the sidelines of the

ballroom, watching the pretty young women twirl and smile coyly in an attempt to catch his eye. He shouldn't be here still, but he couldn't bring himself to leave just yet. He wanted to know that the damn prissy prig, Amity's older brother George, was frothing at the mouth, brought low by a scandal brought on by none other than his own supposedly pure-of-heart sister.

He raked his hand through his hair, trying not to laugh at the truth of the matter. Amity hadn't been pure of thought at all, and had proven herself to be both brave and wicked at once. She didn't even disapprove of his attempts at revenge.

Tomorrow, Roman had planned to present himself at George's door, demanding the debts he held be settled immediately. That should have put Amity's brother in a bad mood, but on top of all this it might kill him. No one could get money from a dead man though.

When it became clear that George couldn't pay Roman off, a pair of Roman's friends were primed to place a wager in the White's club betting book on the likelihood of George Sweet ever having the funds.

Reputations were a gentleman's currency in certain parts of society. Once lost, they forever cast shade on a man's character, and a woman's particularly.

He winced. Amity's would be damaged forever after tonight.

He should feel guilty but could not find it in

his heart. First, it had been by her invitation that he'd ruined her, and by her insistence that he absolutely, under no circumstances, claim to have done the deed. If he were a heartless bastard, he might do the right thing of course and claim her and her hefty dowry. But Amity wanted none of him. He respected that. It was a relief, too. She only wanted out from under her brother's thumb anyway she could think of.

Amity had promised she'd free herself without his blood being shed in a morning duel or having him dragged to the altar and forced to marry.

He admired the hell out of her for making that promise. There were few women who would have in her situation. He was rich enough to be welcomed into many families, should his ambition ever run to matrimony again. Probably not by the Sweets, with their noses in the air at his commoner origins...and George reputedly reading his old love notes to Melody for all to hear.

He ground his teeth and looked around, noticing some women whispering behind fans, swarming together like bees around the sweetest flower, only to then scurry to another group of buzzing women.

Had it started?

It went on like that for a while. The sound slowly rose to a crescendo before some grabbed him by the shoulders to whisper. "Did you hear? Sweet Paragon has been ruined!"

It *had* begun. Roman glanced back at the

speaker, feigning utter surprise at hearing such shocking news. Lord Stratford Sweet, one of Amity's male cousins, was grinning from ear to ear though.

Roman narrowed his eyes. "Should you be spreading gossip about your own cousin like that?"

"I didn't do it," Stratford exclaimed hastily. "George is livid. You should see the scene he's making over in the library."

"Also your cousin," Roman drawled slowly, hiding how he really felt behind an expression of concern. But he turned his eyes toward the far door, hoping to catch a glimpse of his enemy brought low, and of Amity, too. "Why are you not there now?"

"Ravenswood sent me away. One of my aunts has fainted and I failed to catch her. Algernon is trying to take charge."

Roman had not realized the Duke of Ravenswood and his oldest son and heir, Algernon Sweet, Earl of Fairbridge, was in attendance tonight. Roman may not have agreed to meet with Amity if he'd know of their presence. Ravenswood was a cold bastard, but Fairbridge, although quieter than Stratford, was someone a fellow should never think to cross either. He hoped Amity could hold her tongue in the face of that cousin's likely displeasure. "What will be done about finding the fiend?"

Stratford shrugged. "No doubt Ravenswood

will do his best to flush him out tonight so George can have the pleasure of shooting him at dawn tomorrow."

Amity had predicted that possibility, too, and still Roman had gone to her. Helped her ruin herself and enjoyed every moment. He scanned the room discreetly, reminding himself where the closest exit was if a speedy departure became necessary. "Do they have any idea who it might have been?"

"No. Amity's lips are sealed tighter than her legs once were," Stratford muttered coarsely, then chuckled. "I always knew my cousin had a wild heart hidden under all of that prim muslin and lace she wears."

Wild heart, indeed. Roman had never had to work harder to make a lady climax than with Amity in that cramped space. And it had been so worth the effort in the end. She'd come in never-ending waves, rendering him speechless with shock afterward. Hearing her gasp his name and cling to him had made his heart race fiercely.

Too many men rushed to achieve their own satisfaction and denied a woman hers. But the thing that had finally pushed Amity over the edge had been *him*. His cock buried deep inside her, and all while he held her close and whispered sweet nothings in her ear. It was a tenderness he rarely showed his more experienced lovers during their first time together.

Women normally only wanted him for a quick tumble anyway.

Amity had wanted that, too…now to his regret. But there'd be plenty of other women gracing his cock in the future, no doubt. And tonight, he had to behave as he always did. He had to be certain he was never a suspect and end up married or shot or cut to ribbons at dawn. There was still so much more he had to do to make George Sweet pay dearly for his actions. "Surely she wants marriage."

"If she does, she isn't saying so. George probably won't trick anyone into taking her on now, anyway. She's revealed a stubborn streak most men would find unattractive. He's made his displeasure with her behavior well known. Issuing all sort of threats in the hope of loosening her tongue. Fairbridge had to intervene."

That had an ominous ring to it. He turned to Stratford immediately. "What do you mean by that?"

Stratford scowled darkly. "Caught George's filthy paw before he could strike Amity's upturned face. It was almost if she was daring him to beat her. This scandal will end talks of Amity marrying, and after that violent display, my dear cousin might find himself on the outs with society ladies for a while. He's always hidden his brutish nature well…until tonight."

Roman straightened, fury building inside him

unlike anything he'd ever experienced. He'd known George Sweet was a bully for years, especially toward his fellow man, but not when it came to women. And women in his family could never escape such violence when it happened behind closed doors without help. "He tried to strike Amity?"

"The man is beyond the pale. No wonder she's willing to risk being cast out, or perhaps that was what she hoped for."

He craned his neck, hoping to catch sight of Amity. "What will be done with her?"

Stratford merely scratched his jaw. "Don't rightly know. Fairbridge will know what to do, like he always does."

"Get out! Get the hell out!" a man raged, suddenly yelling loud enough to be heard over the hubbub of gossips around Roman in the ballroom.

Roman cocked his head, listening hard. "Was that George?"

"Indeed. There he goes, compounding his sins with a public tantrum, too," Stratford warned. "Why my father ever puts up with the man, I'll never understand."

Indeed, the duke was known to prefer his nephew's company to that of his four grown sons. Roman could not understand that at all. "Maybe this will end his favoritism."

"I doubt it. Father will approve of his rage, punish Amity, and keep us all dancing to his tune until he turns up his toes," Stratford warned, pantomiming puppets dancing on invisible strings. "We'd better go before George *really* starts getting belligerent and shoots indiscriminately at the guests."

Roman grimaced and glanced around. "Does he not remember he doesn't live here?"

"That's what makes him so pathetic. Shall we?"

Stratford slapped his back and moved Roman along with all the other guests who seemed to have decided to leave the ball, too. Or they might be moving in for a closer look at the commotion.

Roman didn't resist going with the flow of the crowd, since leaving was exactly what he should be doing by now. He still looked for Amity through the open library doors, though didn't catch sight of her there. He assumed she'd been spirited away somewhere far from prying eyes to be interrogated.

For a time, they were stuck in the entrance hall, along with everyone else waiting upon carriages. He looked up and spotted George Sweet glowering at everyone from an upper-floor landing, encircled by elder members of the extended Sweet family. Of Amity, there was no sign.

Finally, servants eased everyone toward the front doors with whispered apologies for the untimely end of the evening's festivities. Roman glanced up one more time before he crossed the threshold, his eyes catching George's briefly. His adversary looked utterly unhinged by tonight's events, and Roman felt immense satisfaction, quickly followed by a pang of unease.

What if Fairbridge had not intervened, separating brother and sister when he had? What if Amity was being taken home to await punishment at the hands of such a brute tonight behind closed doors? He was worried about her enough now to consider turning around and doing something rash…and potentially dangerous to his freedom.

He considered owning up.

But Roman was pushed outside, where confusion reigned. Servants struggled to get guests into the right carriages. Roman was pushed forward into one, but when he got inside and lifted his head, he discovered it not to be his. And the Duke of Ravenswood's eldest son was currently in it.

"Begging your pardon, Fairbridge," Roman mumbled, rising to leave again to await his own. "Wrong carriage."

"Sit down, Crawford," Fairbridge drawled. "I'd rather you than my brother, any day."

The carriage took off, leaving Stratford Sweet behind on the pavement, shaking his fist after them. Roman winced and waved and finally looked around. He almost groaned out loud.

Amity was sitting beside him.

He nodded to her, a woman of scandal now. His lovely secret lover. The beauty who had graced his cock so sweetly a short time ago. "Miss Sweet."

"Mr. Crawford," she murmured, raising her chin high and thus revealing the love bite on her neck. The one he'd given her on purpose in the dark under those stairs.

His lips twitched at her proud bearing, but then he quickly schooled his features, lest Fairbridge see his amusement and wondered about it. He glanced at the earl again. "Good of you to take me on. It will save me some time waiting for my own carriage to be found in that hellish crush."

Fairbridge's lips were pressed tight together, and he said nothing in return.

Roman glanced sideways at Amity again in hopes of conveying support and concern for her plight, but she was studying the view out the window as if it were the most fascinating sight in the world. He had to wonder if Amity had any regrets now.

He hoped not, because *he* did not.

When she didn't look his way again, Roman sighed and studied his fingertips until Fairbridge tapped on the roof and gave the coachman instructions to stop. "Well, get out."

Roman nodded to Amity and to the earl, and then climbed out as fast as he could without another word. Worried still for what might happen to Amity later, he considered asking where she was being taken.

But the carriage drove off before he could, turned the corner, and vanished into the dark London night. Roman cursed, and he then looked around properly, quickly discovering his mistake. Fairbridge had left him on the wrong street.

Chapter Four

Amity scowled as the carriage drew away from Roman. "I don't believe Mr. Crawford lives here."

"Doesn't he?" Fairbridge replied with a negligent shrug, his eyes boring into hers.

"No, I heard he resides at the Albany Apartments at present. That is in the other direction, cousin."

"So it is. What a shame," he murmured, continuing to watch her closely.

Amity bore the inspection without fidgeting, refusing to be intimidated by a mere glare. She'd suffered worse at the hands of the tyrant, her brother. "You can leave me here, too, if you like."

Fairbridge growled, and if he hadn't raised his hand, she might have not flinched and revealed her fear of angry men. His eyes narrowed at her reaction, and he lowered his hand slowly. His next words were more subdued than she expected. "What were you thinking, embarrassing yourself like that? Do you realize the cost of your actions tonight?"

Amity took a steadying breath and met her steely-eyed cousin's glare without feeling remorse. He was not like George. Fairbridge had never been violent with her before, or with anyone she knew of, though he must often want to strangle his own brothers frequently. Yet they survived to this day to cause trouble for everyone. But there was nothing Fairbridge, the future Duke of Ravenswood, could do to her worse than her own brother had tried behind closed doors. "Yes. I knew what I was doing."

Fairbridge raked a hand through his hair. Of all her cousins, he was the most similar in looks to his father, the frequently feared Duke of Ravenswood. Dark and dangerous in his own way, and not above putting his own interests first, too. She did not expect leniency or understanding from him.

"Did you not think I could have helped you avoid marriage?"

She blinked, utterly surprised by the question. "Why would you want to?"

"It doesn't matter now, but I was damn well trying," he complained, almost shouting before he remembered himself. He heaved a frustrated sigh and raked a hand through his hair again. "A closer alliance with your brother's cronies was entirely unwanted by many members of the family. I objected to the match, which is likely why George pursued the matter so doggedly."

Fairbridge could be fierce in his dislike of certain people and had become a master manipulator within the family at a young age. George, her brother, loathed his very existence, since he would inherit a title he coveted. But Fairbridge was making a name for himself as a man to fear crossing outside of the family now, too, and George believed his influence was growing too fast to be contained.

Amity supposed she'd made herself his enemy now, as well. She had not intended that but upsetting him was inevitable. "Then you should be thanking me for taking care of the matter for you. Your hands are clean. He wouldn't look at me tonight. I'm sure my brother will never arrange a match between us now."

"Just as well." Fairbridge folded his arms over his chest, studying her with a brooding expression that promised their conversation would continue.

She wasn't sorry for what she'd done. Her ruin and defiance had been liberating. For too long she'd cowered, afraid of putting a toe out of line within the family. As soon as she could, she was leaving London and her controlling family far behind. "Where are you taking me?"

"You'll see." Fairbridge squinted out the window. "You will tell me the name of the man who marked your neck now."

She put her hand over the blemish, not out of shame but out of fondness. She was glad Roman had given her a love bite, something she'd not considered originally. But the way her brother had railed about it so loudly meant that everyone had heard she'd taken a lover. She was grateful Roman Crawford had been so thorough in ravishing her. She'd not had to prove her ruin yet by lifting her skirts for a physician's inspection. She was grateful for that, but it was only a matter of time before her brother demanded her examined to know the truth.

"His identity is my secret to keep."

Fairbridge sighed. "Must be someone you care for a great deal, then."

Fairbridge was far too observant. Yes, she viewed Roman Crawford with a certain degree of affection, but he'd only ever had eyes for that silly twit he'd loved and lost. A woman he continued to pine for in a way that was sometimes painful to behold. She shrugged.

Fairbridge sat forward suddenly. "Was this fellow ever a suitor?"

"No. Merely a means to this end," she promised with a careless wave of her hand, hoping Fairbridge would cease questioning her.

She meant no harm to come to Roman Crawford for what they'd done together that night. He deserved her gratitude, not to become embroiled in scandal with her.

Her cousin's carriage finally came to a complete stop. The grooms jumped down and

Amity quickly looked around to get her bearings, discovering she was not at the ducal mansion where she'd expected she'd be taken for further questioning.

She squinted at the black lacquered door and dormer windows on the high roof of a townhouse she didn't recognize and then looked to her cousin for an explanation.

This was not a family residence. Not his, nor his father's, nor even a meddling aunt's.

A groom opened the carriage door, and Fairbridge climbed out without a word. When he thrust his hand toward her impatiently, Amity slid across the bench and put her hand in his. But she had to admit she was frightened and trembled as he led her away from the carriage and what little comfort she'd found there. "Where are we?"

"You'll see," he repeated.

From his pocket, he produced a key and let himself into the darkened townhouse. A butler appeared out of the gloom carrying a single candle, clearly startled, but welcoming to the late-night arrivals. As if accustomed to this place, Fairbridge led Amity into a nearby chamber and told her to sit down and wait there while the servants quickly lit a few candles.

Amity waited, biting her lip in worry as she took in the unfamiliar surroundings as they emerged from the shadows. The chamber was large and well appointed, the chair beneath her was covered in rich, expensive brocade similar to those found in her uncle's London mansion.

Footsteps came toward them, and Fairbridge turned toward the sound immediately. He disappeared into the hall to meet whoever was rushing toward them. After a few moments of whispered conversation, her cousin returned, bringing with him the woman long rumored to be Fairbridge's lover.

Lady Lydia Barnes was a married woman, and a powerful force in society in her own right. But she had wed a fellow twice her age. Seeing Fairbridge kiss the woman's cheek, while she wore a nightgown and robe, hair tumbled around her shoulders, and knowing he possessed a key to the townhouse where Lady Barnes slept, confirmed their scandalous arrangement was fact after all.

Fairbridge nodded. "I believe you are already acquainted."

Lady Barnes smiled warmly at Fairbridge and then at Amity. She came forward, hand extended to shake. "My dear, what a pleasure to see you again."

Amity had had very little to do with Lady Barnes in the past, but clasped her fingers in greeting and let go quickly. They'd met on several occasions but never formed anything like a close friendship. For one thing, George disapproved of everyone Fairbridge cared for, especially married ladies who might be his lover.

Her cousin abruptly headed for the door. Amity followed after him a few steps. "Cousin?"

But Fairbridge only waved and swept out the door.

"He will return tomorrow at a more respectable hour," Lady Barnes called to her. "Come along, my dear. You must be tired after your ordeal."

Amity's ruin hadn't been an ordeal, but a pleasure. She didn't bother to correct the woman though. What had happened between her and Roman Crawford tonight would be her secret for life. It was a moment she'd cherish no matter what happened next.

Amity held her tongue as she was led upstairs, Lady Barnes taking the lead.

The woman paused at the top of the staircase and moved to link their arms as soon as Amity joined her. "He told me what happened, of course."

"Did he?"

"Indeed, he would," the lady nodded, smiling knowingly at her. "He confides in me about everything that concerns him and his family. I know you've shocked almost every one of them tonight, but not me. He would have made a dreadfully dull husband. They tend to live forever. We have much in common, I think, and I fully expect us to become firm friends."

Amity frowned at the woman and her absurd presumption. A scandal did not make them friends in any way. She was only here because Fairbridge had decided to separate her from the family. "Hmm."

Lady Barnes laughed a merry little laugh as if she encountered ladies ruining themselves to avoid marriage every day of the week.

Amity was shown to a beautiful and richly decorated guest bedchamber.

"You'll rest here, and tomorrow we'll have a long chat over luncheon."

So, she'd be secluded here for tonight, and tomorrow perhaps. Were they expecting her to spill her secrets to return to the family fold? She spared a glance for the high window and noted the sky was beginning to lighten already. "There's nothing to talk about."

"Isn't there?" Lady Barnes smiled, eyes feverishly bright. "I know what you told them—or rather *didn't*—but surely you wish revenge on the man who robbed you of your future in society. You are the niece of the Duke of Ravenswood. Cousin of his heir, the Earl of Fairbridge. The man who ruined you must be punished or brought to his knees in holy matrimony."

Clearly Fairbridge's lover had been denied a complete and truthful account of the events of the evening by Fairbridge and was digging for the truth now.

Amity lifted her chin high and said nothing to incriminate herself or Roman. Lady Barnes could turn out to be just like Roman's spiteful Melody.

Amity loathed women who indulged in intrigue and lorded their power over others. Her brother's wife thrived in society, privy to so much she should never have known, and she made Amity's life a misery at home. Women like that couldn't be trusted to keep any secrets.

"I hold no grudge against anyone."

"Nevertheless, the earl will find the man responsible and make him reconsider his lack of action tonight in speaking up to offer for you. I will now have servants prepare a fire and a bath for you, and provide a nightgown and fresh clothes for you to wear tomorrow, too. Trust me, the bath and time alone will help you decide on the appropriate course of action when it comes to dealing with a certain scoundrel."

Then, Lady Barnes spun out the door and closed Amity inside the cool chamber.

Amity sank onto the bed slowly and eased down to a supine position, putting her head on the pillow above the counterpane. She stared up at the ceiling above her temporary bed while she waited for the servants to come with her promised bath and thought of what the future might now hold for her.

Amity regretted nothing. She would never reveal more about her wild night with a scoundrel to anyone. And as she lay there, she thought of her lover with particular fondness.

She had enjoyed being made love to, and if she were not mistaken, Roman Crawford hadn't disliked having her, either. A pity the circumstances had separated them too quickly. She wished it could be possible to be with him that way again, but that was likely impossible when his heart was still so tightly bound to another lady, and all his affairs since always ended so quickly. He was happier alone and so would she be.

Chapter Five

Three weeks later

Roman paced the Duke of Ravenswood's drawing room, waiting for Stratford Sweet to join him. But as he stood in the Duke of Ravenswood's London mansion an uneasy feeling was growing in his belly.

Amity had *disappeared.*

Utterly and completely.

From the night that Fairbridge had taken Amity from the ball, Roman had assumed her to be staying under the duke's roof until the worst of the scandal had blown over. However, by all accounts, and a discreet question to the Ravenswood butler upon his arrival, Amity was never here. Not since the night Roman had ruined her had she been seen in public by anyone too.

Given her brother was prowling London with a perpetually sour face, he thought perhaps *he* didn't know her whereabouts either.

The night after he'd ruined Amity Sweet, Roman had presented himself at George's door and gone through the motions of his demand to be repaid for debts outstanding. George had blustered about paying, of course, and being too busy to bother with him. Because he didn't pay, a wager had been placed in White's betting book, as planned, causing George considerable embarrassment when he learned of it.

But payment had arrived promptly after that, delivered by so haggard a man-of-business that he was offered a chair and ale and encouragement to unburden himself.

That man of business now worked for Roman, lured not only by an increase in pay and a fine chamber to call his own, but because his efforts were appreciated by a kinder new master who did not yell or throw things across the room.

From the man-of-business, Roman learned that George was still looking for the scoundrel who had ruined his sister. Given all the man couldn't say about Amity's whereabouts, Roman had grown considerably worried about her welfare and eager to learn her location finally today.

He winced. He was a damn fool to be so worried about a woman he'd made love to only once. Amity had brought this scandal upon herself, and yet he couldn't help but be concerned that he hadn't lain eyes on her since. In frustration, Roman had come to his friend's home in the hope of prying some gossip out of Stratford Sweet over drinks that afternoon.

Stratford had always loved to share tidbits of family gossip with him when they were out and drinking together. Amity might not need Roman's help at all, but he felt he ought to be sure that was the case.

He paced the Ravenswood front hall. He was truly worried about what George Sweet might do when he got his hands on Amity again. The more Roman learned of Sweet's ill temper, the more concerned he became. If Amity ever returned to live under her brother's roof, he might make her life a misery…and there wasn't a damn thing that could be done when her family considered her property.

"Crawford?"

Roman looked up into the Earl of Fairbridge's cool gaze.

He quickly bowed to the higher-ranked man. "My lord."

The earl consulted his pocket watch. "Did we have a meeting scheduled today?"

"Not with you. I was just waiting for your younger brother to join me. For Stratford," he added for clarity, since the earl had other brothers.

"You'll be waiting a long time if you linger here." Fairbridge studied him for a long time. Then he tilted his head toward the stairs. "Stratford's chamber is upstairs, first door to the right of the staircase. When he's awake enough to understand, tell him I need a word with him as soon as possible."

He'd known Stratford Sweet a long time but had never been invited anywhere beyond the lower rooms either. "Oh, right. Thank you. I'll tell him to hurry right down."

"I knew I could depend on you not to disappointment me," Fairbridge murmured.

Roman moved to the stairs, taking in his surroundings as he went and trying to slow his thudding heart. There was no reason Fairbridge should suspect him of ruining Amity, but he couldn't subdue the fear of exposure being around any of the Sweet gentlemen.

He glanced over his shoulder as he was going up and spotted Fairbridge watching him ascend the stairs. Roman's skin crawled with guilt. He hoped to God the earl never did figure out who'd ruined his cousin. Fairbridge wouldn't shoot or maim him in a duel of honor. He'd make them marry each other, no matter how miserable Roman might make Amity.

And Amity had been adamant she did not want him for a husband.

Roman found Stratford's door and, after a quick knock from which he heard nothing, he let himself into the room. He found his friend sprawled face down across his bed, half dressed, one of his boots still on.

Roman tapped his shoulder. "Fairbridge sent me up to wake you."

Stratford burst upright, blinking sleep from his eyes and looking around in fright. "I didn't do it!"

Roman chuckled and threw open the drapes,

letting in the sun to warm the room. "You probably did and just don't remember the particulars, like you always don't upon first waking."

Stratford squinted at him. "That was uncalled for."

"The truth hurts," Roman teased with a grin. He'd spent enough time around Stratford to know he could say such things and get away with it if they were alone. Stratford had the most dreadful memory. Everyone knew that, and Roman would use his forgetfulness today to explain his presence. "I believe you wanted to see me."

"Did I?"

Roman nodded. "You sent word we were to meet this morning."

"When? Oh, right. I did. Yes. Now I remember." But he didn't seem at all certain.

Roman nodded again. "Have you asked me to come just to wake you up?"

"No, I…" Stratford thought a moment, and then pointed at Roman. "Hey, you left me!"

Roman drew back, astonished by the accusation. "When?"

"At the ball the other night."

Roman did roll his eyes then. "That was weeks ago."

Stratford sat up, tucking a pillow behind his back and scowling. "Haven't seen much of you alone since that night to berate you for your abandonment."

"You've been busy too," Roman complained. "I heard you've been spending time with the family."

"Not by choice."

Roman spread his hands. "I had no choice that night either. Fairbridge wouldn't stop to let me out of the carriage."

"Sounds just like him," Stratford grumbled. "I suppose you're forgiven. But you weren't left to fight for space to stand up in like I was. I've a right to be cross."

"I'm sorry. It must have been terrible for you rubbing shoulders with the *ton* all alone," Roman consoled, trying not to laugh. "Leaving you behind wasn't my idea, or even pleasant. Fairbridge booted me out far from home and I had to walk the rest of the way there."

"Sounds like something my older brother would do to any one of us," Stratford grinned cheerfully. "Everyone says he was born to be disobliging and surly unless there's something in it for him."

Roman pursed his lips. "He had your cousin Amity with him that night."

Stratford's eyes widened. "So that's how she got away from the family."

Roman was surprised by his not knowing that. "Didn't Fairbridge tell you about taking Amity with him? I assumed he was to bring her here that night on the duke's orders."

Stratford pushed his hair away from his eyes,

blinking quickly. "Haven't seen her here. But I have seen my cousin George, unfortunately. I didn't think it possible for him to look any sourer when he comes around. These past few weeks have been a trial with him always complaining to the duke about her disappearance, and posing all kinds of ridiculous theories to explain it. I though the duke must have had her locked in an attic at first."

"Did he?"

"Not that I know."

"So George assumed Amity was here, too, then?"

"Oh, yes. Of course, when he learned she wasn't, he cursed her roundly. Desperate to find her now, though. Desperate to prove to Father than he's in charge still. He means to fetch her back where he can grind her down under his boot. He doesn't speak very highly about her prospects for making a good marriage anymore."

Roman stiffened. "What's that bastard said about her?"

Stratford grimaced. "Obviously nothing I want to repeat, or that she'd want to hear, otherwise she'd have not gone into hiding, would she?"

"Where could he have taken her? Your brother, I mean."

Stratford shrugged. "I care not. Fairbridge will handle the matter in his own way. Just don't let my father know what you know. What have you been doing these past weeks, anyway?"

Looking for Amity in the face of every dark-haired woman he passed, but he couldn't admit that out loud. He shrugged off his unease at her disappearance and his own obsession with finding her again. "A bit of this and a bit of that," he said evasively.

"I know that look. You've a woman on your mind…or is it the last one still?" Stratford shook his head and rolled out of bed. "When are you going to get over the loss?"

"Never," he vowed immediately. Hadn't they had this same conversation for the last year? Stratford didn't know the first thing about loving a woman when all hope was lost.

"I fear for your sanity sometimes, sir," Stratford complained. "You need someone to turn your head. Even Amity would make a good match for you, despite her ruin. She never revealed her scoundrel's name, so she keeps her secrets and opinions to herself."

"She kept her word," Roman mused—and immediately regretted his praise of Amity's secrecy. *He* shouldn't have known she'd made any such promise to her scoundrel. As far as the world was concerned, they'd never spoken.

Stratford, thankfully, seemed not to have heard and continued to his dressing closet for fresh clothing. He picked out a dark blue coat, fawn breeches, and a fresh cravat. Of course, then Stratford ruined the appearance of restrained elegance by adding a bright green waistcoat that hurt the eyes.

Although he should be above helping Stratford dress, Roman offered to act as valet in the hope of getting him to talk more of Amity. "Another woman is a complication I don't need right now."

"So, there *is* someone on your mind. Thank heavens." Stratford reached for the green waistcoat but Roman handed him a burgundy one instead. Stratford seemed not to notice the difference in color as he put it on and buttoned himself up. "A brief fling is what you need, just the way I like my affairs, too. Satisfactory and blessedly free of encumberments."

"Yes," Roman agreed, knowing it was the expected response. He'd played the scoundrel this past year, as many of his friends did as a cure for disappointed hopes. Seducing women one night and letting them go the next with no hard feelings afterward. Besides, none could claim his heart because Melody still had it. "Your brother is looking for you."

Stratford choked and sped up his dressing. "Why didn't you say so immediately? Let us flee the scene of another likely bad mood and find some pretty ladies desperately in need of manly amusement. I fancy a blonde."

"A brunette for me," he replied, imagining Amity Sweet, her dark hair spilling down around her shoulders, legs tight around his waist as she rode his cock for her own pleasure again. His one regret was that he'd have liked to have seen more of Amity that night. But the shadows had been too thick to even know the shade of her nipples. He hoped to see them still, though…and that was rare for him. Women of late had not stirred any desire in him for a second tupping as easily as Amity had.

Stratford was laughing as he looked up. "That's a first for you. sir, I am very pleased to know you are finally willing to appreciate the other flavors of womanhood to indulge in besides thin blondes."

"Perhaps it's time for a change," he replied with a shrug. Usually, he preferred blondes for amorous company. Melody had a trim figure and was blonde. But after the ruin, it seemed Amity was exactly the kind of woman who appealed to his sensibilities. Of late, she featured in his dreams, too. Of course, occasionally it was with the hint of a nightmare—him on his knees, proposing with a pistol pressed to his temple. He needed to find her so he could stop thinking about her. "Why don't you want to speak with your brother this time?"

Stratford grimaced. "Always pesters me in the mornings. Can't ever let a man sleep late without sending everyone from the pot boy to a best friend to wake me up."

Roman blinked in surprise. "You never said I was your best friend before."

Stratford grinned ruefully. "You're not a bad

sort. We'll slip out the servants stairs to avoid him."

Stratford hurried to finish dressing, and they managed to escape the Duke of Ravenswood's residence without encountering Fairbridge or a single servant who might carry tales back to him.

Stratford hailed a hack and bundled Roman inside. "I have to give my cousin credit. She may have disgraced the family at large, but my brothers and I are still quietly applauding."

The Sweets consisted of four branches. The ducal line had four male offspring, Stratford being last in the succession. There was little chance the other branches would ever inherit the title, but that did not prevent them from playing on their close connection to the duke and scheming for advancement. Amity's line was furthest from claiming the title, and her brother the most envious of all the others.

Roman studied Stratford. What would his friend think if he knew what he'd done? Would he tell, trap Roman into marriage with a reluctant bride. "Amity's scandal is going to make for interesting family gatherings at Christmas. I assume the duke will insist upon everyone attending as usual."

Stratford groaned. "You assumed correctly, and you'll see the scheming and backstabbing for yourself this year, too."

Roman blinked. "I will?"

"That's what I wanted to speak to you about. I

don't want you to make any other plans for Christmas. You're coming home with me. Fairbridge agrees you'll do."

"*Do*?" Roman shook his head. "You want me to join your family for the winter holidays?"

"Why not? It's not as if you've anything better to do." Stratford grinned. "You'd be lonely without me, and you cannot leave me alone to look at Cousin George's face on Christmas morning."

Roman laughed. He only had one brother, and they got along decently well, though they hardly ever saw each other. He didn't mind the lack of censure for the way he lived his life free of encumbrances by family. He earned more than enough grief and teasing from Stratford alone already.

London *was* quiet when Stratford was absent from Town, though. Roman hadn't yet made plans for the distant holiday, and he had to admit that spending it amid the splendor of a large country estate was appealing. Amity might even be there to speak with again.

But so, too, would Melody…and he'd hardly spoken a word to her since her forced marriage. He wasn't sure he should be around her.

He glanced out the window as they came to a halt before the large tavern Stratford favored, and his eyes turned instantly to a dark-haired woman passing the carriage.

No. That was not Amity Sweet either.

They stepped out onto the street and entered

their favorite drinking establishment—The Ruined Spinster. Roman winced at the name as he ducked through the doorway. Ruined spinsters were very much on his mind of late.

They slid into a bench and ordered three ales —one for Stratford, one for Roman, and the third for whoever finished first.

Roman took a small sip of his ale and then asked the question that had been most playing over in his mind. "Do you think she'll return to society soon?"

"Who? Amity?" Stratford shrugged, grinning at a redhead across the room. "I doubt it. She's better off elsewhere, if you ask me. Can't have been easy living with George and his awful bride," Stratford murmured—then looked at Roman in horror over his tankard. "I do apologize."

"For what?"

Stratford winced. "For the fact that George stole Melody from your arms only last year, and even now he must regret it." Stratford buried his nose in his ale, gulping it down quickly.

Roman set his tankard aside, curiosity piqued by the remark about George and Melody's marriage. "They're not happily wed?"

"Lord, no. Melody is…"

"Is what?"

"A damn shrew, if you ask me." Stratford winced, taking another long drink. He wiped his mouth with the back of his sleeve. "Look. Don't be angry with me for saying I think you should consider yourself lucky to have lost her, but you are. I've been present for a few of their dinners lately, and I'm glad it isn't *you* she repeatedly douses with wine at the table for the slightest jest made in poor taste."

"They fight?"

Stratford nodded. "Like cats and dogs."

He shrugged away the matter. If Melody was unhappy, it was all George's fault. "I always found her a sweet, biddable woman."

"That must have been well before her marriage to George. I swear, the servants scatter whenever the pair are in the same room."

He couldn't actually picture Melody angry, but… "She's a right to be angry. He did ruin her."

"Well, they've been married a year already and her temper is still as bad as it was the first day I saw them together. It's a long time to hate someone, let alone a spouse. And it's not just George who she flays with her sharp tongue. She's difficult with *everyone*." Stratford cocked his head. "I never dared say anything about them before because I thought you were better off without her. You seemed heartbroken over the loss."

"I was." Roman sighed. But perhaps not since he'd made love to Amity. He'd not given Melody a thought, really, when he'd learned of George's volatile temper. All of his concern had been for Amity.

Surprisingly, learning Melody was actually unhappily married did not affect him in any way.

He found his lack of care about her odd to reconcile. Most of the last year he'd been obsessed with making George Sweet pay for taking Melody away from him, denying him the love of his life. But when he thought of Melody now…he knew he wasn't heartbroken over losing her anymore. Time and the odd bit of revenge had healed his wound and his pride. Annoying George had become a habit.

"I was *once*," he amended.

Stratford drained his tankard and slammed it onto the table, before reaching for the second with a smug grin. "Good. You deserve better than a shrew for a wife—were you to ask me, which you haven't yet."

"Should I have asked you who I should consider for a wife?" he mused out loud. "Do tell, since you seem to have a wealth of opinion to share today."

"How the devil should I know who you could marry? I'm certainly no matchmaker." He sipped his tankard. "Just make sure she's someone I can like, or our friendship is utterly done for, I promise you."

Roman chuckled softly at the threat. "I'll make sure you approve of my wife, or if you don't, that's it for our friendship then."

"I wish it were *you* who ruined my cousin," Stratford complained, setting his chin on his fist, his eyes showing the effect of the ale already.

Roman choked.

"You couldn't do better." Stratford grinned, sitting up again. "She's all right, our Amity. You know, whenever her brother went out or to bed early, she used to sneak down to join us for a drink and a game of cards late at night. She's a wicked sense of humor, my cousin, wherever she is."

"We've never really spoken," Roman admitted with sincere regret.

"George has a lot to answer for," Stratford muttered darkly. "If he doesn't kill the man who ruined her, it will be a miracle. No wonder he hasn't come forward to claim her. Probably waiting for George to drop dead. We all are."

Discomfort crawled down his spine, and Roman resisted the urge to rub his neck to rid himself of the sensation and accompanying guilt. He could have *not* ruined Amity, but then she'd already be married off to some fat-gut toady George called a friend. He also could have proposed. If he hadn't been so stunned at their lovemaking, he might have considered it more seriously at the time. "What will Fairbridge do? Help kill the fellow, too?"

"Lord no. He'd not risk upsetting Amity like that. She's the only female in the family he can stand. He told me once when he becomes duke, and if he's not married, he'll want her to act as his hostess."

"He likes her? Over all the other female relatives you have? I'd never have guessed."

"He's good at hiding his true feelings about

everyone," Stratford warned. "It doesn't pay to reveal favorites in our family. I don't believe anything until Fairbridge tells me who he likes himself."

Roman stilled as a sudden thought occurred to him. Amity had been with Fairbridge. Alone in the ducal carriage. He'd thought nothing of it at the time. He sat forward, lowering his voice too. "If Fairbridge liked her so much, do you think he would have married her? Before the scandal, I mean."

Stratford skewered him with a hard glare. "We do not marry cousins in our family."

"Many families do," Roman noted, sitting back. "It would keep her dowry in the family."

Stratford shuddered and took a long draw from his tankard. "We don't think of her that way. She's almost a sister."

Roman let out a relieved breath. At least he was reassured that he'd not come between Amity and a brighter future as a duchess.

Stratford made a show of checking his pocket watch. "I'd best get home soon. There's a cousin due to give birth across town and everyone's probably pacing the halls, waiting on the messenger to arrive, wringing their hands as if they're about to become fathers themselves."

Roman laughed softly and shook his head. The Sweets worried about a lot of things Roman never had to think about coming from a small family. But fatherhood was a daunting prospect for many men. He'd been lucky so far not to have fathered a brat on any of his past lovers. But the thought of Amity big with his child made his heart shrink with fear…and for some strange reason, a yearning to see if she was increasing. It shouldn't happen. He'd withdrawn and not spilled his seed with her.

But what if Amity, despite his care, might somehow conceive?

She was cut off from her family, spirited into hiding by Fairbridge, who might not treat her kindly should she be found with a bastard growing in her belly. For his own peace of mind, he really ought to make sure that Amity was not increasing. "Could she be at the duke's country estate? Amity, I mean?"

Stratford took a deep drink of his ale. "I know for a fact Amity is not. Nash has just returned and made no mention of it. But that does not mean she's not at an estate belonging to Fairbridge. Do not tell anyone about my suspicions on that, either."

"Never. Has he many properties?"

"One I suspect not even Father knows about yet." Stratford glanced to the side to where Roman's tankard sat neglected. "You're not drinking with me."

"Letting it breathe," he assured his friend.

"It's ale, not fine old wine, my friend," Stratford complained.

"True enough." Roman took a hasty gulp of

his forgotten ale and then signaled to the barkeep to bring three more tankards, which he happily paid for. If Amity wasn't here in London with her family, or at the duke's country estate, she might have been taken away to live out her days at Fairbridge's property. A property not well known to the rest of the Sweet family yet.

Was it possible to get Stratford drunk enough that he'd tell Roman everything he knew about Fairbridge's investments?

Chapter Six

Amity lifted her face to the cloudless sky, drinking in the warmth of the beautiful summer morning. Loving her new life.

She was free.

Living in a quiet village in the country these past weeks suited her much better than the crowded ballrooms of the marriage mart she'd been trapped in for years.

For a moment, she considered what her overly fussy female relations might say to see her in her current condition. Hair imperfectly bound, no bonnet covering her head, muddy shoes, and a hem sadly very much blemished. A certain aunt and Amity's sister-in-law might just faint at the poor impression she was making on the residents of her village, many miles from the heart of London's glittering Mayfair ballrooms.

Amity much preferred the honest reek of the countryside, though not the pigsty she was currently passing on her way to the center of town. The pomanders and perfumes of the truly well-bred members of the aristocracy tended to be as much more on the nose. Like the pigs, too, society was full of wind.

She continued down the muddy roadway from the cottage Fairbridge had sent her to where the townsfolk perpetually gathered each morning. There was so much to be seen and so many people to meet.

Amity hitched her basket higher on her hip and wove through the crowd of locals, speaking to those she knew by name and nodding to others still wary of her, a stranger in their midst. She was known as a married woman here, rather than a ruined spinster. As a wife who'd abandoned her marriage when her husband had been unfaithful.

Some of the women didn't like her simply because she was pretty. She'd turned heads upon her arrival, and on any given day she might see a fellow lurking outside her garden gates in the hope of escorting her somewhere, ignoring that she was already spoken for.

Amity encouraged none. Not that a few handsome souls weren't worthy of consideration, but because she had a pretend husband somewhere, of course. And her heart had been unexpectedly claimed, too—despite her best intentions not to fall.

Roman Crawford would never know the impact of the brief time they'd spent together. He, despite his affection for another, had become the man of her dreams.

A middle-aged bachelor, perhaps the most

prosperous of the local gentlemen, strolled up to her with a beaming smile of obvious delight at seeing her out and about. "A right pretty sight you are today, Mrs. Standish. I was just thinking to myself that you were missing out on so fine a morning, and I no more than turn my head and see such a vision coming toward me."

She inclined her head to the man. "Good morning, Mr. Fletcher. And where is your dear mama today? Somewhere nearby, I expect."

Fletcher drew closer, wincing. "Her hip aches badly again, and so she must remain indoors."

"Oh, I'm sorry to hear it," Amity murmured. Mrs. Fletcher's hip seemed to ache badly with increasing frequency since Amity had first made her acquaintance, and her invitations to take a private tea with the woman were increasing apace. She was sure now the older woman, who had once gone everywhere escorted by her dutiful son, was now making herself scarce. Amity wasn't sure the older lady entirely believed her story of being a married woman, because her son always approached her with a proprietary air, offering to protect her from those he considered unworthy.

She looked over him again and noted the speculative gleam in his eye was there again. "I mustn't keep you then, sir. I know Mrs. Fletcher depends on you above all others for company during the day."

Fletcher stretched out a hand toward her,

imploring her to stay. "Perhaps you might favor her with another visit?"

Amity kept her hands at her side rather than encouraging any physical contact. She was a properly respectable wife, in every regard except for abandoning her pretend marriage. "Not today, I'm afraid. I have quite the list from the Misses Beamish. They've still a sniffle and cough to be taken care of. I've become quite worried."

"It's good of you to do so much for them. A sign of your good heart, caring so much for near strangers," he nodded approvingly, looking around, likely to see who was watching them speak as he so often seemed to do. "I'd best not keep you."

She curtsied to him. "Thank you. Enjoy your day, Mr. Fletcher, and my best to your mother for a speedy recovery."

Fletcher let her go without another word and Amity let out a soft sigh of relief. Not having a husband underfoot, even a pretend one, was proving more of a problem than she'd anticipated it could be.

As a married woman who'd abandoned her husband after a terrible fight, she was somewhat scandalous, though she made sure to never let the proprieties lapse around any man. Unfortunately, she now seemed to have become a target for many gentlemen hoping to enliven their quiet lives with a clandestine affair. Amity rebuffed them all, but at least Mr. Fletcher might have honorable intentions toward her. She couldn't imagine his mother would allow him not to. He was quite under her thumb, in her opinion.

From the gossipy baker, she bought fresh bread; the barrel-sized butcher sold her a large joint of smoked ham to make into broth or soup; and from the flower seller, a posy of violets to put on her neighbors' sickroom side tables. She moved past the sweet maker but paused at the stall of a bookseller. The Misses Beamish were bored with their illness, and she'd promised them a new story if she could find an affordable volume.

The old man's eyes lit up with recognition and not a little hope. "Can I help you, madam?"

"Perhaps."

She perused his collection, noting many of the same books he'd had on display last time remained on sale again. But she spied a book of poetry she'd admired before and purchased it, mostly to give him at least one sale today. The locals were not much for reading but the Misses Beamish liked to listen to her read aloud to them often. This small book of poetry would be perfect for many occasions.

She thanked the bookseller, told him she hoped to see him again next time, and turned away, only to run into a broad, manly chest clad in rich blue velvet.

The man mumbled an immediate apology—and she looked up into Roman Crawford's laughing eyes.

"Roman!"

He stepped back and offered an elegant bow. "Miss Sweet."

"Shh," she hissed, praying no one had heard him speak her real name. She lived here under an assumed one, mostly for the fun of it but also to throw her brother off her scent, should he ever stir himself from London to look for her here. She'd wanted to cut all ties with her family, even with Fairbridge, who'd generously offered her the cottage to live in with no strings attached. "Mrs. Jane Standish."

Crawford's brows drew together. "Who the hell is that?"

"Me. Now."

He rolled his eyes. "Of all the ridiculous choices you might have made. You are most definitely not a plain Jane."

"Keep your voice down!" Face heating a little, she hastened to move away from the bookseller, who'd started watching them too closely for her taste. The trouble with being a stranger in a small town was that everyone wanted to know everyone's business, especially hers.

Crawford hurried to catch up with her. "Where are you going?"

"I was intent on enjoying market day until you arrived. That is what village women do on days like these, you know."

"Ah," he said slowly, then surprisingly offered to carry her basket for her.

Amity handed it over, planning to make good use of the scoundrel by purchasing more than she could reasonably carry by herself in one outing. Since coming here, she'd been very frugal with her funds. Fairbridge had added a generous sum of money to her traveling trunk before she'd left London but had sent no more, although he'd promised to continue funding her living, provided she cause no further trouble for the family.

At the time, she'd easily accepted his terms, and the cottage to live in, because her brother had been a beast she feared going back to. So, she'd lived here anonymously for the last weeks, striving to make a home and new friends, using an assumed name and invented past while making sure every penny spent was on necessities only.

Books were surely a necessity for living happily anywhere.

That might all unravel too easily, now that Crawford had come. Had he reconsidered the appeal of her dowry? Had he told Fairbridge he was the one to ruin her and been sent here to fetch her back and marry her?

Amity increased the distance between herself and Crawford, glancing discreetly about them to see who was near enough to listen in. "What brings you to this part of the countryside, sir?"

His brow rose. "Concern."

"Concern? For whom?"

Crawford smiled tightly and looked around

them, too. "For you, of course. You disappeared without a trace."

"Not well enough, it seems, if you found me so easily," she muttered under her breath.

He shrugged. "It's been weeks. It took time, and a great deal of ale poured down your cousin's throat."

"Which cousin?"

"Stratford first, and the others to a lesser extent later."

She regarded him warily. "Why would you care so much about where I'd gone?"

Crawford swung the basket by his side a few times, silent for a long painful moment, and then he pointedly lowered his gaze to the region of her belly. Her flat belly. He didn't look at her as he spoke. "Since I did not see you again after that night, I was left to fear there might have been a complication to your plan. A consequence that you shouldn't have to face alone."

She blinked rapidly, the sharp pinch of emotion catching her by surprise. She had wondered if she might conceive after their one brief tryst, too. But her courses had come exactly on time after that night with him, and carrying a child of his wasn't a remote possibility now. "You worried about me having your babe?"

"Very much." He pulled a face. "Of course, I wanted to know that you were well after your first time, too."

"Very well, and very grateful." She raised her

hand to her throat, relieved he hadn't followed her for her dowry alone. "The mark you left upon my neck was proof enough of my wickedness that I was spared the need to submit to a more... intimate inspection."

He gaped. "Your brother demanded you examined?"

"Not him, but my aunt suggested it might not be a true ruin. I feared George would want proof before he believed my tale entirely. A doctor would have been sent for eventually. Probably my cousin Nash Sweet, to keep any scandal quiet and in the family. That was why no half measures were possible. I had to be bedded thoroughly, beyond a shadow of a doubt."

She looked up at his face, and saw Crawford's expression was now set in murderous lines.

She put a restraining hand on his arm, fearing an outburst. "Everything that happened after you, I expected to happen."

"Well, I did not expect this at all for you." He threw his free arm out wildly, encompassing their surroundings. "The indignity of you being sent away and the threat of having your cousin look up your skirts cannot be borne. I ought to wring his bloody neck!"

Although she flinched inwardly at his wild gesture, she made herself remain still. "Calm yourself, Crawford," she whispered, even as she nodded to a passing local who regarded Crawford with barely concealed interest.

"I'm sorry, but I cannot do that."

She looked at him sharply, hoping he'd not cause a scene here in public view. "You must, for my sake if nothing else. There's nothing you could have done. I was happy to leave London and reconciled to proving my ruin. But the unpleasantness is behind me now, and I can be at peace at last."

"It is wrong that you are not living the life you were meant for. You're not even being yourself."

"I am more myself now than I have ever been," she promised, telling him what she had always believed about her life in London, as she'd told herself those first nights when she unexpectedly experienced doubts. She had not been her real self in London, except for the one glorious night when Crawford had made love to her.

The pretend part of her life was over. This was better, even if pretending to live as a married woman with an absent husband meant she might never marry anyone at all or have the children she'd always imagined doting on. "Mrs. Standish lives a respectable life alone."

Crawford made a grumbling sound, and then thankfully fell silent on the subject.

She studied his face carefully, wishing peace for him, too. While it was to his credit as a gentleman that he cared enough about her to seek her out, it changed nothing for Amity. Crawford was even more handsome than she remembered, but in love with someone else. She tried to take her basket from him. "It was good to see you again."

"Not so fast. I still have your basket to carry for you."

Although Amity reached for it again, he would not give it up. So, she had no choice but to continue with her shopping, and have Crawford keep her company. Even when she stopped to purchase ribbons, he never once complained she was taking too long. He stayed close. Watchful but seeming in no hurry to leave her, now that he'd found her safe and well.

As she browsed and bartered for her purchases, she cast an occasional glance toward her companion. It was hard to believe so confirmed a scoundrel had actually been worried enough about her welfare to follow her here, of all places.

Done with the market, she returned to his side and added her last purchases to the basket he carried. "That's everything I need."

"So, tell me about your Mr. Standish," Crawford asked in a low tone. "Is he somewhere about?"

"No." She wet her lips and hid a smile. Standish was a figment of her imagination. "My *husband* and I quarreled over his affairs, and I left him wallowing in some harlot's petticoats. I am quite done with him."

"I don't blame you at all." Crawford grinned, catching on quickly and lowering his voice. "You keep the advantage of having a living husband somewhere to protect your reputation without having to deal with one underfoot. Very wise of you."

"I thought so." She'd modeled her husband's behavior on Crawford, right down to his continued infatuation for her sister-in-law. Of course, she'd changed everyone's names and places of residence.

Crawford nodded. "So, can I assume he's a stranger in these parts, like you are, too?"

"Yes, but I describe him very well, and most of my new friends agree I'm better off without such a man in my life."

"What do the rest of them say?"

"That he'll come to his senses one day, mend his ways and come crawling back. All philanderers feel a need to be reformed by their wives, or so I'm assured."

Crawford rubbed his jaw. "They do say reformed rakes make the best husbands. In the end, after a period of reflection and penance." A huge smile burst over his face, making him even more handsome. "Will you make him suffer and grovel? Bring you flowers and wait on you hand and foot?"

"I hadn't considered the possibility of groveling obviously, since he doesn't exist," she mused. "But I suppose some would be expected for me to ever speak to him again. He broke my heart with his scandalous betrayal."

"I'm so sorry."

"Why should *you* be sorry?" They had finally reached the gateway to her neighbors' home, and she paused to study Crawford one last time. Her heart skipped a beat. He'd found her, she'd answered his questions, and now that his curiosity was satisfied, they could say goodbye and he could be on his way.

She curtsied and took her basket from him. "Thank you, sir, for your company and concern. As you see, I am quite content. I trust that you will have a good journey home to London again and a happy life. Please *don't* give my regards to my family."

Crawford squinted at her a long moment but then reached for her hand. Amity's heart started to pound as she unthinkingly extended hers to be claimed. When he pressed a long kiss to the back, she relived some of the sensations of their scandalous night together. His tenderness had affected her then. It still did now apparently.

He glanced up, grinning, and she knew he'd sensed her unspoken response to him. "Until we meet again, sweetheart."

Amity walked away from him on trembling legs, ignoring the urge to look back over her shoulder for one last glimpse of her tender lover. It had been astonishing to see him again, but of course that part of her life was over. Now that she'd satisfied his curiosity about how she'd fared, he would forget her and return to pining for her horrid sister-in-law.

That certainty, above all she'd been through, was the one thing that always made her sad when she thought of him.

Chapter Seven

Roman shook his head as Amity Sweet swept away from him without a backward glance. Who did she think she was fooling with this act of hers of being a common country wife?

Amity Sweet was extraordinary in every way possible. Gracious, charming, and more attractive than was good for him. There was no way to mistake her for anything but a member of the aristocracy. From the slightly haughty tilt of her head to the way she glided everywhere as if her feet didn't quite touch the ground she walked upon.

And the damn woman affected him more than she should, too. He already ached to kiss those sweet lips and taste her soft skin again.

She might just be aching for him, too. He'd heard the catch in her breath as their hands touched. Glimpsed desire brightening her eyes when he'd lifted his head after he'd kissed the back of her hand, too.

It had taken him so many weeks to pry her location out of her unknowing relatives without giving away his keen interest in her welfare and whereabouts. He'd not bothered to enquire about Amity to her older brother though. Clearly George had no idea of her location, or he'd have fetched her back in the blink of an eye to bind her to another man in unholy wedlock. And he knew that to approach a man he despised to ask after his sister might have caused suspicion to fall his way about the wonderful night, mere minutes, they'd spent together.

But if anyone could have hidden Amity's location so well, it had to be done at the behest of her cousin Lord Fairbridge. He couldn't be applied to directly for information, of course, but his brothers were not so suspicious of casual enquiries made of their relations, given they'd discussed others in the past ad nauseum while deep in their cups.

Eventually, by asking enough of the right questions discreetly, he'd pieced together the extent of Fairbridge's private holdings within any short distance of London and had slipped away from Town to visit each area in turn.

He had just about given up the hunt when he'd happened upon Amity standing at the bookseller's stall.

His heart had done an uncharacteristic flip at the sight of her animated expression as she'd bartered with the merchant for the slim volume, oblivious to his scrutiny.

She looked happy. Happier than he'd ever seen her, in fact.

He should have spun on his heel then and there and departed, considering his mission complete. He'd found her, and she was clearly well. But he'd experienced a compelling yearning to talk to her again, though his stomach had churned with the uncertainty of his welcome.

And when she'd looked up and smiled, he'd become utterly and completely charmed. It was not every day a woman ruined welcomed the return of their secret lover with such a forgiving smile.

Now that he'd found Amity safe and content, he ought to leave her to her peace and go back to London to make merry again with his friends and continue to wreak havoc on her brother's life.

Except…he didn't want to go just yet.

He had not expected to find her on the first day here, so had already taken rooms at the village inn. His men and horses were not in the village with him though. He'd left them behind at a farm to mend a cracked wheel, where he'd paid for their stay with a generous handful of coin. They were all weary from his seemingly pointless travels anyway, so he'd promised them a few days of idleness after the repair was done while he'd rode ahead alone to scout the area.

He'd spoken with the innkeeper of this charmingly rustic village about his keen interest in purchasing an estate here, but hadn't given his name yet. The man had assured him there were properties to be considered and would act as his go-between with local landowners if he was in earnest about any.

To leave without meeting with at least one might arouse suspicion. He had the perfect excuse to linger, so why not pretend to be an investor up from London and spend more time with Amity, if it were on the cards? They had not parted as enemies, after all. They were not friends, either, but something that he couldn't quite put a name to yet.

Roman wandered the market, watching the townsfolk come and go. It was an interesting place, a tidy cobbled square with a well and clearly prosperous population. But it was a place unbefitting a gentle beauty like Amity to settle down in.

Queen of London society Amity ought to be, in his opinion. Something more than a supposedly betrayed wife of a man no one had ever met. It was a clever ruse, and one few here would likely directly question her about to prove her tale true or false. But any husband of Amity's would be a fool to betray her with a woman of lesser standing.

Society loosely applied the term incomparable to young wide-eyed girls fresh to the slaughter of the marriage mart. Amity might be older but was the embodiment of the term still. Bold but graceful, accomplished but modest. If not for meeting Melody first, Roman thought he might have paid attention to Amity in London.

If not for her horrible brother, they might have danced, come to know each other better.

But he'd only been given one chance, and that was to ruin her. He might be disgusted with himself if the lady had not been the one to extend the invitation. He knew he'd done her bidding, a service, been chosen for his skills as a lover and also for his unavailable heart and deep pockets that didn't need refilling. And for weeks, he'd told himself repeatedly that Amity was better off not being associated with him at all, should she ever return to London. Her scandal had died from the lips of the gossips already. They had forgotten to wonder about her disappearance in the wake of all the other juicy scandals continually taking place in society.

But he couldn't do that—forget her.

Amity ought to be back in society, where she belonged.

He scratched his head. Somehow, ruining a sweet lady had changed his mind about where his loyalties ought to lie, too. He'd had a lot of time to think while away from London. Revenge was all well and good, but eventually it no longer provided Roman with sufficient satisfaction. Melody was married, and her husband, if he'd not suffered a seizure yet after all Roman's machinations and schemes to destroy his peace, seemed to be in continuing perfect health. Roman couldn't even claim to be heartbroken.

He was finally free of the past and ought to give more thought to the future.

Roman was certain that if he wanted to consider himself a gentleman and a good man, he should take this one last chance to know Amity better before it was too late. There was no one here to get in his way, as there would have been in London.

There was no better proof of his change of heart about the women in his life than the fact he hadn't taken a lover since Amity, too. He'd had plenty of offers and sly invitations from wives, widows and even a debutant or two. But none had compared, or tempted him away from thinking of his missing lover.

It was Amity he wanted to make love to.

If she'd ever have him without dire need forcing her hand, that was. If the circumstances were right and he could protect her reputation, Roman would be more than happy to be hers again.

She exited the house she'd just entered after a brief visit, and he admired the way she moved, shifting her emptier basket on her delicate hip. Rather than follow too closely and cause alarm, he merely watched her from a distance as she walked down a lane and entered another small cottage and didn't come out again.

A desire he'd never expected to feel so keenly after Melody beset him as he considered knocking on Amity's door just to see her face again.

To distract himself from doing so, he purchased a pair of oranges to eat as he enjoyed the summer day. He studied the house Amity had disappeared into and saw a curtain twitch at an upper window. Was that her new home?

He turned to the fruit seller with a question. "Is there much to see down that way?"

The fellow looked him up and down. "Traveler from London, are you?"

"Indeed, I am. I am in search of a property to purchase if I can find the right one." He pointed past the last row of houses. "Unfortunately, I don't know the area all that well, but it seems a pretty place. Could you tell me which estates are down that way?"

"Lord Barnes has an estate a bit farther along that's for sale, and until recently he owned most of the cottages on the other side of the roadway, too," the man confided, pointing to the last cottage Amity had disappeared inside of.

"Ah," Roman said, nodding. The last pieces of the puzzle clicked into place. Fairbridge must have made the purchase of the cottages from Barnes and had whisked Amity quickly out of London to live in quiet obscurity.

Roman did not agree with that decision at all.

Roman asked more particulars about the area. He learned that a Lord Barnes' had an estate that was sorely in need of repair. Lord Barnes' wife was rumored to be Fairbridge's mistress which might explain why Fairbridge owned property here, too.

He asked if there were other properties of similar size about the area, just as another man turned up at Roman's side. They eyed each other. Given the quality of his clothing was very good and his bearing proud, he was perhaps the richest man in the village. The fruit seller introduced him as Fletcher.

"A few," the Fletcher drawled, butting in. "There be a good view of the district from atop that hill. It's not long till sunset though. You can see for miles and miles to get the lay of the land. The innkeeper can arrange an appointment with any of the stewards of absent landowners for you."

"Ah, excellent. Thank you."

A sudden idea struck. He'd like to take in the view and watch the sunrise with someone by his side. He couldn't ever have asked a spinster to take an evening walk with him without a chaperone present. But to everyone in this village, Amity was known as a wife.

If anyone saw them together then, they wouldn't care as much as they might had her real identity and circumstances been known.

But there was another way that guaranteed her reputation wouldn't be harmed.

"I say, do you know if there is a Mrs. Standish living somewhere in these parts?"

"I couldn't say," the fruit seller replied, glancing at the other man with a frown.

The man's face became closed off. Almost hostile. "I don't believe I caught your name?"

Roman held out his hand. "*Standish.*"

The fellow's eyes rose impossibly high on his face as he gaped. "Standish, you say?"

"Yes, indeed," he promised. Amity had left a scoundrel of a husband to live here. He could very well be that man for her. "I'm quite keen to be reunited with my wife after so long apart. Have you met her?"

Fletcher seemed to swell, and Roman became alarmed when he drew closer and growled, "You are Mr. Standish? A man who betrayed his own wife with her relation?"

Clearly, Amity had painted a grim picture of her husband and had found a champion in this fellow. Was he a suitor, too? Perhaps he thought he was, but Roman couldn't see them together as a couple. Even scandalously.

Roman straightened to his full height as well and looked Fletcher in the eye. "That is between my wife and I, sir."

Sensing an unwinnable dispute in the wind, the fruit seller wisely placed a restraining hand on Fletcher's shoulder. "She's in the last house, on the edge of the village, sir."

"Thank you," Roman replied with a sincere smile and regal nod. "I'll call on her shortly, after speaking with the innkeeper about a viewing."

It was dishonest and presumptuous to pretend without consulting Amity first, but he would pretend to be her Mr. Standish, come to woo his reluctant wife back to their marriage. If he failed

—and the odds were not on his side—there would be no harm done, really. No one here knew what her husband looked like because he didn't even exist. If he kept the lie simple, he would likely be believed.

And if he played the part of her husband convincingly well, it could only solidify Amity's claim that she was truly a wife.

Chapter Eight

Amity startled at a loud knock on her front door in the late afternoon. The hour was unusual for callers, especially on market day. She threw a shawl over her shoulders and shoved her feet into her half-boots, quickly tying them in place so she looked somewhat respectable again.

But sometimes a local woman did visit her late on market day, often to escape a boorish husband deep in his cups. Sometimes it was just a gardener from the manor house come to look for a stray cow in her garden.

Her solitary maid was currently preparing her dinner at the back of the cottage, so she answered her front door herself, expecting to see a friend.

What she found was the old bookseller from the market, regarding her with a delighted grin as he swept his hat from his head and bowed. "Madam, I hope you don't mind my unannounced call today, but as a lover of books, I hoped to gather your opinion on a volume of poetry that fell into my hands. It was after your visit to my stall, or I would have shown it to you then and there. Might I come in to show you?"

Amity glanced beyond him and thankfully could see no one else watching their exchange. She could not invite this stranger into her home, not without a servant present to protect her reputation. That would be unseemly and cause harmful gossip. She'd worked too hard on her ruse to see it spoiled by carelessness.

But Amity *was* interested in books, so she stepped out her door and shut it firmly behind her. "I should be very happy indeed to discuss your new book. May I see it?"

The bookseller picked up a leather satchel from beside his feet, then looked up at the sky. "Perhaps we might go somewhere with shade."

She nodded and led the way to a shaded patch of ground near her garden gate.

"I must say, your presence has been a breath of fresh air to the district," he confided to her with a smile.

"You flatter me."

"No. No. Business is booming thanks to your discerning purchases over the past weeks," he promised. He produced the slim volume with a flourish, handing it out to her to view.

She picked it up and opened the pages. But then she frowned as every page she turned revealed to her a book she'd seen before. *At his stall.*

Amity nearly rolled her eyes at his pretense in calling on her. Did he think her so dim-witted not to remember his small collection? No doubt, he'd come in the hope of selling her another book today. She handed it back to him promptly. "It's very nice but I have read it."

"It's a very fine edition," he promised with a keen smile as he stroked the binding while holding it out to her. "I think if we were to go inside, perhaps, we could read this together. You must be very lonely without your husband's company after so long."

Amity gaped. From the remark and from the nerve of the old man to make so bold a suggestion. But just as she was about to blister the fellow's ears with all manner of insults, a whistle drew her attention. Someone was coming down the lane at the worst possible time.

She prayed that they would see the bookseller at her door and not recognize the nature of his visit for the scandal it clearly was.

The whistle grew louder, and Amity swept around the bookseller to stand by the garden gate to put more distance between them. The relief she felt upon seeing Crawford headed in her direction, though, tossing a pair of oranges into the air, defied belief. She awaited his arrival breathlessly, aware that the bookseller had followed her to the gate as well.

Crawford's brows rose high when he noticed the other man behind her, but he continued to toss his pair of oranges into the air. "I'm afraid I only have two."

"This gentleman was just leaving," Amity assured him quickly.

The bookseller made a sound of protest.

Amity turned to him with a sunny smile. "Thank you for the view of your book. I'm sure you'll find a worthy home for it very soon."

The bookseller seemed inclined to stay, but eventually snatched up his satchel and headed back to the village marketplace.

Crawford watched him go and then tossed her an orange, which she only just managed to catch. "For your supper."

"Thank you," she murmured, keeping watch on the bookseller's retreat. Of all the nerve to assume she was lonely and wanted *an old man's* company! She would never have invited him in, and she might never grace his bookstall again, either.

Crawford's eyes narrowed, and then he looked over his shoulder and back to her again. "Was he bothering you, sweetheart?"

"No." She nibbled her lip. So far, she'd been deft at deflecting unwanted attention from gentlemen because she claimed to have a husband somewhere. But she supposed her ruse could only last so long. She'd always had her brother or her family name to protect her from opportunists and true scoundrels. She feared the bookseller might even come back. Obviously he was very lonely. "He *might* have become a problem, had you not come along when you did," she admitted reluctantly.

Crawford turned and flung his orange at the

bookseller's back. "Don't let me see your face again!" he cried out in a huge and startlingly loud voice.

Amity noticed with some satisfaction that the bookseller definitely hastened his escape, grinning when he was out of sight. "Thank you for that, but you shouldn't have."

"It was a pleasure to protect you from a scoundrel, especially an old one." Crawford offered a flourishing bow, and then dug in his pocket and produced a single flower to hand to her. "Something to brighten your afternoon."

She was truly touched by the gesture and lifted the flower to her nose. "This is just what I need to lift my spirits after that interview."

He smiled so warmly that her toes curled in her boots. "Madam, I've come with a proposition that might lift them even more."

"A proposition for what?"

He pointed behind him. "A stroll up that hill. I've heard from the very best source that the grandest views are to be had from up there."

Amity considered going along but quickly changed her mind. It was too great a risk, even if she thought she might really enjoy spending more time with him.

He leaned close. "If you're concerned about any impropriety, I'll have you know I've taken any number of strolls and carriage rides with married ladies with no one thinking much of it."

She drew back from him. “That is an unpleasant thing to say to me.”

“It shouldn’t be, since you’re pretending to be a married woman yourself.”

“Ah, I see.” She felt like such a goose for not remembering some of the rules no longer applied to her. “I did not think of it quite that way when it came to you, though.”

He beamed at her and held out his arm. Since she’d already closed the door to her cottage, and dinner wouldn’t be ready for some time, she accepted his offer of escort without a qualm now. She slipped her arm through his and showed him to the beginning of the upward slope. “I’ve never dared go up by myself.”

“But you’ve gone with others.”

“No. But others go all the time. Especially courting couples.”

“Perfect,” he said, beaming her another smile. “We shall enjoy our first look at the district together. It seems a pretty place from the lower ground,” he noted.

“I agree. I must admit, I was very pleased that Fairbridge sent me here rather than to the ducal estate.”

Crawford nodded. “He sent you to be near his lover’s husband’s estate.”

“I’m not actually sure they’re lovers,” she hastened to say, wanting to speak no ill of her cousin. “But they did seem very close.”

Crawford patted her hand. "Must be, if he took you to her home the night of your ruin."

She looked at him in surprise. "How did you…"

"I told you. I asked better questions than your brother ever did and figured it out," he assured her.

They were silent for the climb and at the top, they were both a little breathless after the steepest part. "The view is spectacular," Crawford exclaimed, walking about with his arms wide.

Amity laughed at his enthusiasm, caught up in it. "You don't get this sort of view in London."

"Or Wales, which is where I'm from, by the way. London does have its charms, though."

She stared at him in surprise. "You live in Wales?"

"No, I came from there. My older brother has the family estate now, and I live wherever I please these days."

"Do you miss them? Wales and your family."

"No. Can't say that I do. The only thing I truly have missed was seeing you in London."

She grinned at his ridiculous statement. "I am surprised you even noticed I was gone. You never paid me any notice before that night."

"I was wrong to have let my anger with your brother narrow my view so much," he said as he came close. "I'm done seeking revenge against your brother, by the by."

"I'm glad to hear it. I'm sure you enjoyed his

frustration but there are other things in life worth your time, I'm sure."

Roman smiled down upon her. "So there are…and I'm looking at one right now."

Amity gulped as his smile made her wish for things currently beyond her reach. "My brother's rage was spectacular. I'm sure he lost a great deal of support in the family, given the way he carried on."

"And so did you with many, too," Crawford murmured, a look of guilt in his eye.

She was touched by that but shrugged it away. "I knew it would happen."

"But never will you lose my admiration. You have become luminous." He cupped her face tenderly, his eyes soft and compelling. "My secret lover."

"You're mine, too."

He nodded and bent his head. "Let's not be strangers another moment longer," he whispered, and lowered his head until his lips stopped just beyond reach. "May I kiss you again?"

Amity inhaled his scent, reveled in the tender touch of his hands upon her face. And then she raised her chin until their lips brushed, pulling him closer.

The kiss seemed endless, and Amity was clinging to Crawford when he finally pulled back.

He grinned. "As lovely as the first time."

Amity pulled away from him. "I'm sure I hardly compare."

"To whom? Widows and bored wives?"

She turned her face down to study her fingertips. "To her. To your Melody."

Crawford slipped his finger under her chin and lifted her face to his, and held her there gently, commanding her complete attention. "I want you to listen to me very closely. Never have I *ever* thought of her while I was kissing you…or thinking of kissing you."

Amity met his gaze warily. Such a declaration made her heart very glad. But just because he could set aside his feeling for Melody to be wicked didn't mean he had come to care for her anywhere near as much. They had been lovers, and might be again one day, but that was far different from actually having any real claim on his affections.

She shrugged. "I…"

"Do you really believe another woman played a part in those few glorious minutes we spent together in that cramped closet?"

"I want to believe she did not," she admitted. "But you *were* seeking revenge against my brother."

His fingers closed about her skull, holding her fast so she could look at nothing but him. "If I went with you seeking revenge, I'd have married you to claim your dowry for myself, whether you liked it or not. I have never needed a wealthy bride. And I have not turned the countryside upside down for the last weeks looking for you, only to upset *him*, either."

He settled his lips on hers again, and she fell into his arms completely, sure of his intent at last. He wanted more, just as she did.

He took his time kissing her, seemingly in no hurry to be done. But eventually, he turned her in his arms toward the setting sun, so they could watch it sink below the horizon together.

Amity sighed when it was over and turned to look up at Crawford. "So why did you really come back to see me? I thought you would already be on your way back to London."

He seemed to hesitate. "Can I explain that when I call on you tomorrow? I promise to give you a full account. However, I think it best to get you home before full dark, so we don't get lost together."

"Might be a good idea." But she was dying of curiosity. Had he really missed her so much? Or was it his conscience that had played a hand in his search for her across the countryside? She did not need his pity. It was too much to believe that he might have come to care for her after so brief an affair.

Crawford peered out over the landscape one last time, and then down toward the village to establish their bearing for the decent. "Beautiful. Tell me about your life here? Do you like it?"

"Very much indeed. The locale and villagers are truly pleasant."

He nodded. "Any would-be suitors I need to know about?"

"How could there be? I'm a respectable married woman."

"So you are. But that does not matter to some fellows."

She pulled a face. Fletcher. The bookseller. Any distant farmer come to town always seem to find their way to her door. "There are a few who perhaps might look at me a certain way, but I have never encouraged any of them."

"Good."

And then took up her hand and peppered her with questions about the weeks they'd been apart on the walk downhill. Especially about her deception and the tales she'd spread about her life after coming to live here. At no time during the descent did he let her hand go, until they reached the front door of her home.

She was rather breathless, from the exertion as much as his attentiveness. She would have liked to have invited him inside, too. Liked him to stay to take dinner with her and talk some more about his life. She'd never had a chance to speak openly with him in London. Her brother would have forbidden any association between them at all because of Melody. Most likely, this was her only chance.

However, before she could decide how to broach the subject of Crawford coming in, he bowed deeply, thanked her for the gift of her company, and then headed immediately for the village inn, which was the only place he could be staying overnight.

Amity walked inside her cottage and shut and locked the front door behind her, and then stamped her foot for the lost opportunity. It always seemed too short a time with Roman Crawford. And now it was over again before she was ready again. Tomorrow, he'd come to take his leave of her—likely for the last time.

Chapter Nine

Roman was decidedly nervous as he headed out of the village inn the next morning as the sun rose, best coat on and his cravat perfectly tied. He'd never actually ever gone courting. Not even with Melody. They'd seemed to fall into each other's orbit at a country ball, and he'd never considered not being with her when she'd pleaded with him to follow her to London while she enjoyed her first season.

But his pursuit of Amity was the decision of weeks of separation and silent deliberation on what was right for him, and for her.

Yesterday's kisses had only confirmed his suspicions that a longer-term connection with the beauty was his heart's deepest desire.

His vagabond existence couldn't continue forever. He could not drag Amity from place to place and expect her to be happy. It was time to put down roots at last. Settle down. Marriage, children, and decide where to call home. Clearly, he didn't love Melody anymore. He wasn't sure Amity could ever love him though. But he would see what she had to say and eventually propose, only so long as she wanted him the way he was. He couldn't change the past. He held grudges, hated her brother, and had once been in love with her sister-in-law.

That might be too much for her to forgive.

Thinking back, he easily recalled Melody's fascination with society upon her arrival in Town, and her thrill at meeting so many new and important people. She'd loved the attention and had become swept up with the excitement of her first season. So much so that Roman had felt a little sidelined more than once. Then, he'd never thought about the future.

But he was now.

He would not make the mistake of trusting that love could ever be easily won again, or kept.

He arrived at Amity's garden gate, breathless and more than a little nervous. He should have told her about his change in identity yesterday, but he had been hesitant in case she'd be angry and refused to see him again. He would have to tell her today before someone else did, and see how she viewed the decision he'd made without consulting her first.

He knocked sharply on her door and stood back, ready to wait an hour even to be received. He'd never felt that way about any other woman, but he knew that here was where he was meant to be right now.

When she peeked out the curtain beside the door, he grinned and wedged his hat under his arm. In his other hand, just out of her sight, was a bunch of flowers, which he'd purchased the prior day and kept in water in his room to keep them fresh overnight.

The door opened wide. "You're up early!"

"These are for you," he said, thrusting the flowers at her and hoping they were acceptable.

She gaped at him but took them with a nervous smile.

"I have found the answer to our problem," he murmured.

She looked at him with suspicion. "To what problem are you referring?"

"The problem of how to see you again, and alone, and not ruin your reputation a second time. I'm currently pretending to be your scoundrel of a husband, come to win my reluctant wife over. Might I come in?"

Her lips parted in a gasp but no sound came out at all.

To be honest, after a few minutes of that he became a bit flustered that she didn't readily go along with his scheme or say no to it.

Though, it was a bit of a wild one, even for him.

She regarded the flowers in her hand, frowning down at the bunch. "Yes, I think you'd best come in, sir, to explain yourself."

He crossed her threshold, relieved to have made it this far, and looked around immediately in case there was a servant hovering nearby.

Amity marched away from him. "Mary, would you put these in water and prepare tea? I have an unexpected visitor."

A young woman with dull brown hair poked her head around the distant doorway, mouth agape as she took him in.

"That's him," the woman whispered to Amity. "The one who was asking about you in the village."

"Yes, I'm sure it was. Never mind that now and do as I ask."

Mary looked around Amity and gave him a once over. Roman pegged her immediately as something of a town gossip. Not five minutes after she finished for the day, the local women would hear about Amity's visitor. Wonder about him. Speculate and spread the word until eventually everyone would come to believe Roman was Amity's scandalous husband in the flesh.

Once the locals put his face to her husband's name, she should never be bothered again by scoundrels who came knocking on her door.

Amity turned back to Roman.

Aware that there was still someone else in the house, Roman kept up the ruse of a husband come begging and gripped his hat in his hands tightly. "I've come to ask you to take me back."

Amity rolled her eyes. "You know it's too late for that."

"It's never too late when there's love," he swore, leaning into his part as best he could.

Her eyes closed briefly as the maid appeared with the bouquet of flowers, now in a water jug for a vase. The maid fussed, and when Amity opened her eyes again, she seemed near to tears. She even sniffed as she sank into an armchair. "But you love her."

He reeled from Amity's display of heartbreak and hurried to sit on a stool near her feet. He drew on his experience with Melody to form an appropriate answer. "She's married now, and likely never not to be," he promised. "But that's over and done with. I only have eyes for you."

The maid smiled as she fiddled with the placement of the vase across the room, making a show of separating out the stems—all the while watching for Amity's reaction to his pleas for a second chance.

"I want to believe you," she whispered.

"You know you can," he promised. "I learned my lesson, sweetheart."

The maid swept from the room at last and then there was silence.

Amity scowled at him fiercely. "This farce is beyond the pale."

"I think it suits both of our needs," he promised in a low tone. "We could have a splendid few days together, and then have a row or something else dire could come between us to send me on my way again."

Amity raised her finger to her lips, cautioning him silently not to say another word.

He'd no intention of having any sort of serious row with Amity. But he did need time to prove himself worthy of a second chance. He was confident that if they spent time together, if he courted her, she'd discover he was more than just a means to an end.

The maid returned quickly, bearing a tea tray and a plate of biscuits but it was obvious she was straining to hear every word they exchanged.

"Thank you, Mary. I'll see you tomorrow," Amity said firmly, dismissing her servant, and then stood when the woman left the room.

She went to peek out the windows and looked outside.

"Finally, she's gone." Amity turned about, hands on her hips. "So, you want to spend a few days pretending we're husband and wife? Why? Just for the thrill of it? Are you mad?"

"Not that I'm aware of," he said, fighting a grin. He quite liked Amity's fire, little seen until this moment.

"And what sort of woman would I seem to others when I send you packing again? A woman too weak to deny her husband's appeal. A woman easily swayed by a handsome face."

"You could bear it very well if offered the right incentive. A few days by your side, and nights spent in your bed, and I'll prove my worth to you."

She shook her head. "What purpose does this serve? You avoided becoming embroiled in my scandal once already. I'm not with child, so you can set your mind at ease about that. No one would have possibly suspected you of ruining me until you showed up here, uninvited. Why do this?"

He rushed over to her but stopped a foot away. He bent his head, grinning from ear to ear. "You want everyone to think you're married, and I'll help you convince everyone."

She gasped and drew back. "You *are* mad."

"What harm could come of it?" he confessed. "If you intend to stay here forever, I am perfectly placed to help you establish a proper past. They don't know me either."

Amity moved to the table and made an attempt to pour tea. However, her hand seemed to be shaking, so much so that she made a mess before rushing away.

Roman waited patiently for her return, and she came with a cloth in hand to mop up the spill. She dropped into a chair again and he moved to sit across from her and studied her calmly before he poured the tea himself.

Amity put her head in her hand, watching him.

She had clearly not considered that he could help make a marriage seem real between them. She might even enjoy it enough to want to keep him. He was filled with hope for that outcome but he would accept what ever she decided, of course.

Amity attracted him for lots of reasons.

Perhaps it was because she didn't expect anything from him at all. Perhaps it was because of the way she had kissed him back, too lustily to be ignored too.

But whatever the reason for his fascination, he intended to see this through. Pretend to be her husband to spend time with her. And if his courtship failed to support the idea of them actually marrying, well, they'd stage a public quarrel, and he'd say farewell to Amity once and for all.

"I want you to hear me out. If I am known as your Mr. S, your neighbors will have a face to put with the name of this imaginary husband you created. They'll never question his existence, and I'll make damn sure every single scoundrel—and bookseller—knows not to come knocking on your door again."

"But you're not my husband. You're Roman Crawford. If the innkeeper knows that, then everyone does."

"I did not want anyone to know I was looking for you, so I did not give my name when I took rooms."

"But your grooms on your carriage know your real name."

"My grooms are five miles away, no doubt drunk or sleeping. They'll never come here. I can let it be known that I was a man traveling discreetly so my flighty wife couldn't escape me again."

She stared at him. "Oh, that is almost believable."

"I got the idea from you," he told her with a wink. He sipped his tea, and Amity did as well.

"Flighty?"

"I hoped it would garner me more sympathy from other men to describe you so."

Her eyes narrowed. "You've introduced yourself as my husband to the men of the village already, without asking me first?"

"Indeed. Last evening, before I called upon you I met one Mr. Fletcher, a man of obvious importance and wealthy. He displayed a possessive sort of interest in you that I didn't care for. I put him back in his place."

A soft smile trembled on her lips. "Fletcher and his mother have been the most suspicious of my marital state."

"Fletcher didn't seem to care for my arrival. Just how big a scoundrel has your absent husband been?"

"I found you in bed with a relative of mine."

Roman set down his cup. "Naked?"

"Naked," she said firmly.

He grinned. Amity had imagined him naked, and weeks ago, too, it must have been. He schooled his features. "Do go on. I need to know how big of an idiot I have to play."

"I never said you lacked wits. You were drunk at the time, though. In my story."

He shook his head. "I must have been, if I wanted to take any other woman to bed but you."

Amity sat forward and regaled him with all the horrible things her husband had done to humiliate her. By the end, Roman felt quite uneasy… because the details were not so far from the truth of his life. There were some events she mentioned that had actually happened to him with other women, although some were greatly embellished to make them seem more sordid. He cleared his throat. "All of that was after Melody."

"I…" She reached for his hand. "I am not criticizing your behavior."

"Are you sure?"

"Yes, but what I know of your life did help make my story more believable. You are real to me, and so I could describe the scoundrel in you very well."

"I'm glad I could be so memorable."

Amity pulled a face. "Although, after what I told everyone about how you hurt me, I will have to ring a peal over your head should you ever look twice at any women in the village."

Roman lifted Amity's hand, which she seemed to have forgotten he was holding, and brought it to his lips. "I'm only here for you, sweetheart," he promised in a whisper. "No one else. How exactly was I making love to that other woman?"

"The way we were. Under the stairs." She blushed. "I only had the one experience to relate about lovemaking."

"I'll give you a dozen more before too long if you agree to take me back," he vowed. "There are countless ways to make love, and I intend to show my wife each one in exquisite detail as I plead my case." Roman continue to kiss up to her wrist, but her long sleeve prevented him from higher exploration. He tugged her up to sit on his lap and looked at her face. "So, what do you say? Can I be your pretend husband? Yours until dawn?"

"Husbands don't usually leave their wives at dawn, you know," she warned.

"Well, I didn't want to assume you'd make it easy for me. I've a lot to make up for."

"I could be mean to you, I suppose," she agreed. "Make you work hard to win me back."

"I'm willing to work as hard as I can to please you. Between your legs, too, if you'll let me."

Her gaze softened and her breath caught.

He leaned close to whisper, "Do you want to be made love to today, sweetheart?"

She caught her lip between her teeth as she considered his offer. "Yes," she whispered somewhat breathlessly.

"Anywhere I choose to have you?"

She nodded very fast then.

He grinned and brushed a stray strand of hair from her face. "Multiple times, starting with here on this very chair."

Her eyes widened slightly in shock and her mouth formed a perfect o, but she did not say no to him. In fact, she seemed aroused by the idea.

"I'll take your silence for a yes, until you say you don't like it this way." Roman adjusted Amity until she straddled his lap as if she were riding a horse. "My one regret was that I couldn't see you when we made love that night."

"It was mine, too. It seemed like a dream after."

"I'm no dream, but flesh and blood and hungry for you." Roman settled his hands on her thighs and slowly worked her skirts above her knees. It could have been the work of a moment to bare her legs, yet he took his time. He'd rushed the night of her ruin, but he was done with doing things in a hurry when it came to intimacy with Amity.

Her legs were slim, the lower half encased in serviceable stocking instead of silk, with short, well-worn boots on her feet. Her pretty knees and thighs were bare. He stroked them with just his fingertips.

He loosened his breeches as his cock swelled, mostly for comfort, but did not reveal himself to her yet. He slipped his hands under her gown and teased her inner thighs.

"You should make good use of your husband while he's here, my sweet," he whispered as he dotted kisses on her cheek and her neck. "I have much to make up for, and I've neglected my wife badly, haven't I?"

She choked on a laughed. "I suppose you

have. It's been weeks since I've had any attention to my needs."

"I'll never leave you wanting again. I mean to lavish my wife with all my considerable skill in the bedchamber and beyond too."

Amity groaned, and he pulled her head down and stole a proper kiss from her lips, all the while watching her expression as he teased his tongue into her mouth.

She wriggled closer and looped her arms about his neck, clinging to him the way she had in the dark closet under the stairs. But the closer they got, the sooner this tryst might be over.

He leaned back and strummed his thumb across her nipples lightly. Watching them harden beneath her gown made him harder, too. He wanted to see her body. Since the lacings of her gown were at the back, he settled for tugging her gown off one shoulder to reveal one perfectly shaped breast. Her nipples were a soft brown, pebbling further in the cooler air of the room.

He blew softly across the peak, making her gasp.

"Crawford!"

"Husband," he corrected.

"Husband," she said, sighing with what distinctly sounded like pleasure. "Must you always shock me?"

He slipped a hand under her dress and cupped her sex, making her gasp even louder than she had the first time. He chuckled softly at her reaction.

"It seems your lot in life to have a rake for a husband."

She wriggled again on his lap, and suddenly he was the one gasping out loud. Amity had slipped her soft hand between them, into his open breaches, to pull out his cock.

Roman groaned as she started to stroke him with just enough pressure to curl his toes in his boots. "You seem more educated than last we met," he managed to gasp out.

"Wives discuss their sexual conquests," she whispered in his ear, causing a shiver to race through him, especially when she nipped his ear with her teeth. "I'm keen to put what I've heard into practice with you."

She'd learned very well indeed. "I'm more than happy to be fodder for your continued stories if this is how you practice the carnal arts."

Not wishing to be the only one on the brink of an orgasm, he carefully slid a pair of fingers inside her, making her rise off his lap briefly. When she sank back down, it was with a rather desperate gasp of pleasure and the loss of her hands on his cock.

She'd forgotten him, and he didn't mind. Her touch had been alarmingly arousing as she'd stroked him. He kissed her throat, determined to focus on her pleasure first. "Have you been dreaming about me being inside you, sweetheart?"

"Every night since," she vowed, rising, only to sink down on his fingers again. He encouraged her to continue. "So much better." Her movement sped up as she impaled herself, gasping a little louder each time.

"Better than what?"

"My memory and attempts."

The image of Amity, legs spread in her lonely bed, fingers dipping between her lower lips while she thought of him, was too much. He removed his fingers and fitted her to the head of his cock immediately.

They both groaned, and as she sank down, he met her gaze. A blush colored her cheeks and her eyes were wide as they started to fuck each other. Though the chair creaked beneath them, Roman was confident it would hold in the face of such blinding lust.

Amity came first, and quickly, crying out as she shuddered and clawed at his head, pulling him to her bosom.

Roman tongued her nipple but roared out his release a moment later, unable to stop himself climaxing inside her body. "Amity! Am—"

When it was over he kissed her fiercely, knowing their first time together hadn't prepared him at all for the passion to be found in her arms again. He'd never felt like this about anyone ever before. Not even with Melody, and he'd thought theirs was true love.

He could not walk away from this woman. Not until he had purged her from his soul or claimed her heart entirely.

Since Amity lay huddled against him on the chair, he pulled her to him properly and rose. Holding her with one arm, and the other hand holding up his breeches, he carried her off to her bedchamber to make love to her until dawn.

Chapter Ten

Amity was so confused by Crawford. He said he was only pretending to be her husband, but when she lay in his arms, it felt so perfectly natural between them. Is this what a casual fling was supposed to turn into? The talking and tenderness and the wanting that never seemed to end.

She hadn't ever imagined it could be like this with any man. Certainly, none her brother had introduced her to in London.

Crawford, *Roman*, had made love to her last night and each time she thought it was over she craved to have him again. The first time on a chair, which she now blushed to recall, had been the right beginning. She might never sit in that room again without thinking of it or him. The second time they'd made love had been in her own bed, and Roman had left her weak and trembling and she'd fallen asleep without knowing it.

She'd expected him to be gone before dawn, but he still slept at her side even now. She glanced over her shoulder at him. Quiet, handsome, everything she craved still.

Roman slept face down, completely naked under the bedsheet. She remembered making a detailed inspection of his entire physique when they'd first come to her bed. Roman had laughed but indulged her curiosity. He'd lain back, one hand pillowing his head, and let her have her way inspecting his front side. His amber eyes had danced with amusement in the candlelight until the moment she'd asked him to turn over. But he *had* turned over, his muscles flexing with the effort.

Unfortunately, he could only bear her kissing down his spine for a few minutes before flipping over, capturing her, and kissing her witless. They'd made love for what had seemed like hours after that. She could hardly recall the evening without her cheeks heating anew. Was her reaction unusual or did all women react this way to him?

Although she'd like to talk to him about the pleasures they'd shared, she wasn't quite ready to voice them yet. She had so many questions and thoughts on what they'd done last night, and what they might do next if he wanted to share her bed again.

If.

She sighed. It was still very early, and she was loathe to wake him up. Last night had been exhausting—especially for him, given the way he had flipped her this way and that, supporting her body weight as they made love all through the night. There was still plenty of time for him to leave before full sunrise yet, or perhaps he might stay and make love to her again. She'd like him to stay. Perhaps longer than he might want to, though.

Her stomach suddenly gurgled its need for nourishment, and since neither of them had eaten last night, Amity carefully climbed out of bed and drew on her nightgown and then grabbed her largest and warmest shawl to throw around her shoulders. She crept from the room as silently as she could and pulled the door shut behind her. She wanted a cup of tea and a chance to think about what she really wanted from Roman Crawford before the maid came to start her day.

She ought to feed Roman too. She wasn't much of a cook, but she could at least heat water for tea and toast stale bread on the fire if hers could be stirred to life.

She glanced out the window, just able to make out the shape of the nearest houses. All were dark still and she saw no one out and about, so she let the curtain fall again. By now, the villagers might have heard that Roman was her husband and would likely see nothing wrong with him spending the night. They would imagine they'd made up and resumed their marriage, along with all the usual benefits of one. She had to admit that so far, the benefits had exceeded her expectations. Her new friends in the village would probably approve of their so-called reconciliation. They had all cautioned Amity not to give up on her marriage, or her handsome husband.

But Roman would leave, and then what would they think of her? She'd be blamed for driving him away. He surely must go, though. He had a life elsewhere to live. Her brother to torment. Another woman to mourn the loss of, even though he claimed to be over her.

Amity might have found Roman's revenges alarming in the beginning, but she had seen a certain rightness in them in the end. George had used Melody's ruin to line his own pockets. He'd claimed her, and she suspected George had somehow managed to extort money from her family, too, to keep things quiet. And George had continued to laugh at Roman's loss for all to hear in public, setting him up for ridicule by others. All of it within Melody's hearing but the woman had never once protested or asked him to stop. She remained silent, complicit. Allowing a good man to be maligned.

It was one of the reasons Amity could never truly think of Melody as a sister. She seemed to enjoy living in the center of a difficult situation. Roman deserved far better, in her opinion. She hoped when he returned to London that he might find other interests one day.

Amity padded silently through the house. She knew all the spots where the floorboards creaked and protested her slight weight.

She went to the room where she and Roman

had first made love and quickly tidied the space, pushing their chair back in line with the rest. Satisfied there were no clothing belonging to either one littering the floor, Amity headed for the kitchen—but found the maid already there an hour earlier than she ought to be.

Amity winced inwardly and adopted a happy outward mien. "Good morning."

The maid looked up from stirring the fire to life. "Good morning to you, too, Madam. You're up very early today."

"Yes, I couldn't sleep and came to make tea," Amity said quickly, feeling her cheeks warming with a blush as she thought of the man asleep in her bed. "Have you been here long?"

"Not very long but I'll have tea ready in a moment."

"Thank you." Amity smiled and glanced around discretely. As usual there was bread for toast, and cheese already out, too. Easily enough for one hungry lover.

The maid straightened and dusted off her fingers, a look of worry on her face. "I couldn't help but notice you didn't eat the food I set aside for your dinner last night. Was it not to your liking?"

"I'm sure it was but I found I wasn't hungry then." She'd had her fill of her pretend husband instead. He was all she was able to think about last night. She prayed he did not come stumping down the staircase at any moment, looking for her. She'd be embarrassed and married women were not supposed to be embarrassed by having entertained their husbands.

The maid brightened. "Would you care for porridge this morning, perhaps? Can't have you fading away to nothing. You must be famished."

She had no idea if Roman liked porridge, but Amity was hungry enough to eat last night's supper, and porridge, too. "Yes, please."

"It won't take too long."

Amity, however, hovered at the kitchen doorway, watching the maid set out a meal and listening, dreading, hearing movement from above or the direction of the stairs behind her. When the maid paused, clearly almost ready to serve her, Amity cleared her throat.

"Mary, why don't you take the day off."

The maid looked at her in surprise. "What for?"

"Surely you'd rather be doing something else than scrubbing dirty pots in my kitchen."

"Not really. You're an easier employer than my last," the maid promised with a broad smile that fell away just as suddenly. "Begging your pardon. I shouldn't have said that."

The maid had come with the house. Fairbridge had hired the local woman, so Amity knew little of her past. "Who did you work for before starting here?"

"I shouldn't say, madam."

Amity took a step into the room. She

absolutely hated it when she didn't have the whole story spelled out to her. "Mary?"

The poor woman looked decidedly nervous, but eventually she shrugged. "I'd worked for the Fletchers since I was a girl."

"They've never mentioned it."

"Likely not. Mrs. Fletcher got the idea in her head that I was making eyes at her son, and he with me."

"With Mr. Fletcher?"

"Yes, madam. But it is not true. He would never look at me the way he looks at…" The maid shook her head. "He's a great man, Mr. Fletcher. Far too far above the likes of me, I know. He would never want me that way."

"Mary, who do you think Mr. Fletcher does favor?"

"You." The maid stilled and kept her eyes downcast. "He would make any woman happy, I'm sure."

Amity moved into the room and sat at the kitchen table. She sensed in the other woman bitterness she knew only too well. Had Mary developed real feelings for Mr. Fletcher over the years of her employment, despite claiming that she had not? "Mary, I'm a married woman."

"I know that now." The maid peeked at her under her lashes, eyes flashing anger. "But in the beginning, it seemed…"

From that look, it was clear the woman had

not ever believed her story. Might never have, actually, which made Roman's arrival well timed.

Amity gestured behind her. "For heaven's sake. My husband is upstairs, in my bed, right this very minute."

The maid's eyes widened. "So, you forgave him?"

"Not completely. That is why I am giving you the day off. We have much to talk about, my husband and I, before I can forgive him," she assured the woman. "He did betray me."

The maid chewed her lip. "Are you sure you should be alone with him today, madam?"

"Quite sure. My husband is not a violent man. Unfaithful, yes, and he knows I won't forgive him easily after the humiliation he dealt me. But what we discuss is between us alone." She definitely wanted no one to interrupt her and Roman because she hoped to find out how long he might stay and how often they might make love in that time. "I'll manage everything else on my own, I promise, and see you tomorrow morning as usual."

She made a shooing motion with her hands, and the now grinning maid bobbed a curtsey, removed her apron, caught up her shawl and slipped out the back door. When Mary smiled, she was remarkably pretty. How typical of a man like Mr. Fletcher not to notice he was loved from afar in vain.

Amity heaved a sigh, committed now to this

wild tale they'd concocted together. She was the wife with a husband who had to be accommodated, and made to suffer, too. He should probably move his possessions from the inn to her own home sometime today, too.

She had to admit, she didn't mind having Roman for a husband at all. He made her crave things she hadn't known existed. She could easily become addicted to his kisses, and that made her feel decidedly weak around him.

"Is everything all right?"

Amity looked up with a smile on her lips, so glad to hear his voice again. She rushed to kiss him. Roman was only partially dressed, standing bare foot in her home. She took in his lean rumpled form and her heart flipped in excitement for what might happen between them today. "Are you hungry?"

"Starving for you." He captured her and held her close. "I woke to find you gone."

"I'm hungry. After last night…"

"Lovemaking does work up an appetite, doesn't it," he murmured before nuzzling her neck, as had become his habit. He moved past her into the kitchen. "Is there any tea?"

"Yes, and porridge soon, too," she promised, rushing to the pot to stir it.

Roman followed and peered over her shoulder into the pot. "Ah, your maid has been here, has she?"

Amity frowned and stirred some more. "I could have done it."

Roman scowled. "I would hope you didn't have to. That would be the last indignity I could bear if you were forced to cook your own meals. Your cousin should have provided sufficiently that you never needed to toil in any kitchen."

Amity laughed at his protest. When she'd first arrived, she had wondered how severe her banishment would be. However, she'd been met by a couple who acted as housekeeper and gardener. They came by once a week at her request. "He did provide me with staff. But I've reduced the hours of toil for all he employed, mostly on account of their ages and my lack of need. I want to learn to cook a little, too. Just the necessities, you understand."

Roman lifted the heavy kettle steaming over the stove and filled a delicate teapot set on the worktable. Amity stirred the porridge again, but it seemed little improved by doing so. She should have asked Mary *when* it would be ready before sending her away. It was too late to call her back now though. "I don't think this is done yet."

Roman looked over her shoulder. "Agreed. You'll have to suffice to satisfy my hunger."

He swept her away from the stove and dropped her onto the edge of the kitchen table.

Amity looped her arms around his shoulders, laughing in surprise. "We could go back to bed while we wait."

"Why go anywhere else?"

"Well, we could talk, or make love there."

"Who needs a bed when this table right here seems sturdy enough to hold the two of us." He kissed her cheek. "What was it you wanted to talk about though?"

Amity bit her lip a moment and then decided there was no point in waiting for a better time. "Are you leaving today?"

"No," he promised. "Unless you've had enough of me."

"I haven't," she said softly. It was nice to have Roman here, nicer to have his arms around her still. She made her shawl fall off her shoulders and pulled on the drawstring at her neck to loosen her nightgown. "I'd like you to stay and make love to me again."

Roman nodded and wrapped her tighter in his arms. He was warm and so familiar now. She heaved a sigh and rested her cheek upon his chest. His heart beat loudly, keeping time with hers. "I didn't expect you'd stay the night."

He kissed the top of her head. "I didn't mean to but I'm glad I did to see you this morning. You are utterly beautiful without all the frills and starch you used to wear."

"My aunts controlled my wardrobe. They never listened to what I wanted to wear." But she thought of what he said about her attire. He liked her as she was now, not as the primped and polished paragon. Of course, it might also be that her nightgown was rather loose, and he could peek down the front of it to see her breasts. Amity could feel herself becoming aroused and heated just from knowing he might be looking at her nakedness. "How will you spend today?"

"With you, I hope," he said as he cupped her breasts in his big hands. "There's not a lot to do in this village unless its drinking at the inn or indulging in gossip."

She shook her head. "They will gossip about me now."

"About us, as I had intended from the start." His fingers eased down her torso to her sex, pausing, maddeningly, just above where she'd already begun to crave his attention. His fingers slid from side to side, teasing her with the anticipation of his tender touch. "I would never again neglect such an incredibly giving woman."

She stilled his hand. "Crawford, what do we do if the maid comes back?"

"You told her to go and why. If she disobeys and see us together like this, it's her own fault for interrupting a married couple making up after a long estrangement. I am quite prepared to be seen making amends, too. Your husband was in the wrong. A fool to let you go," he promised as he urged her to slide farther up the sturdy table. He pulled off his shirt and tossed it carelessly aside. His bare chest and shoulders gleamed in the morning light.

Wearing only his breeches and a cheeky smile,

he set his knee on the table and crawled up to join her, holding himself over her—caging her between his strong arms and thighs. He hovered there, his expression one of utter mischief. "I must say, I like pretending to be your wayward husband. Satisfying all those urges you've only just found existed has become an ambition of mine."

She squinted up at him, walking her fingers down his chest toward the bulge in his trousers. "How do you know I didn't have those urges before you came along?"

"I hope you did, but now I have to hope those thoughts are for none but me. I want you to only think of me when you're being truly wicked."

She studied Roman and decided there was no point denying her attraction and interest in him. They were lovers. She wanted them to stay lovers for as long as he could bear being away from London. "Perhaps I did and *do* think of you. Perhaps I always could, if given the right incentive."

"Then let's not waste another moment more making up." He lowered slightly and skimmed his lips over hers. And just like the first time together, everything fell into place, and they didn't need to say another word about what they expected from each other. "I want you to always think of me and what we do together."

Amity was in complete agreement. She tugged her nightgown up to her waist and out of the way, and eased her legs apart, making room for his body to fit snugly against hers again. Just as she'd started to wish it could always be between them. Natural and easy and exciting and tender. She kissed Roman with all the passion she felt, all the love that only seemed to grow deeper the longer they spent together. She was completely committed to her lover and hoped to be forever in his arms.

Chapter Eleven

Despite his best efforts, Amity stirred as Roman tried to slip out from beneath her as gently as he could. He kissed her brow and moved her onto the mattress beside him, then considered covering her up to her neck because her pearly white skin was such a distraction. He became so easily aroused seeing her this way. Their lovemaking in the kitchen had been fun but he preferred seeing her lying in her own soft bed, sated, after a day of love play. He wished they could stay like this forever—except, he had an appointment arranged for this morning.

Curiosity was getting the better of him about any other Sweet family business he might have stumbled upon.

"I'll be back in a few hours."

Amity slid her leg out from under the sheet, toe pointed and seductive as she wiggled it at him. "Do you really have to go?"

He spent a moment considering, grinning at her flirting with him. "I've turned a paragon into a wanton woman. Not that I'm complaining. It's my pleasure to make you happy, my dear." Roman laughed, kissed the top her head and rolled out of her bed. "But unfortunately, the innkeeper might send out a search party if I don't make an appearance at the inn soon. I wouldn't want anyone but me to see you like this."

Her eyes sparkled as she held the sheet across the lower part of her face and batted her lashes like a coquette. "Do I look like I've been ravished?"

"All night long," he promised, full of wonder for the day and night they'd shared. They were so in tune when it came to exploring their passions. Hungry and willing to do anything to please the other.

As he gazed down upon her now, his cock stirred yet again, eager to sweep them into another passion-filled encounter that would last for hours. But he always kept his promises. That meant appearing to go about his declared business of finding a property to purchase, and to be seen about the village as her husband, too.

He was sure now that their passion wasn't a once-felt stirring but something that could be built on and explored for the rest of their lives.

He stood up and padded around her tiny bedchamber, picking up his clothing and putting each piece back on. Every time he drew close to Amity, he stroked her skin…her bare legs, her arms, the sweet dimples on her lower back when she exposed it to escape any accidental tickling.

In time, this woman would be his to love

every day if he was lucky. But he still had to convince her that marriage to an enemy of her brother's was worth the risk of lifelong estrangement from them all. He also wanted her to return to society, as well.

It was a shame that he'd never have her family's approval to marry her. George Sweet surely had wanted Amity to marry someone far more distinguished than a mere mister with deep pockets. The Duke of Ravenswood might disapprove the match very vocally, as well, and challenge the marriage. Although Amity was over the age of consent, there was still the possibility that he might yet face pistols or swords at dawn and end up leaving her all alone again.

Amity deserved to marry whoever she chose, someone she loved, and by God, she could have him if he could secure her heart, too.

With that thought in mind, as he pulled on his boots, he considered exactly how to go about declaring his honorable intentions. He would have to speak with the duke. Ride to London or visit his country estate to speak directly with Ravenswood himself. It was an interview he very much dreaded but felt was entirely necessary. The duke could be quite vicious and unforgiving to those he considered had wronged him, but he was the head of Amity's family.

Roman might also have to explain why he'd lied to Ravenswood's sons, apologize, if he wanted to stay friends with them. Stratford particularly might take issue with him ruining his cousin, even though he'd said he wished Roman had been the one.

"Roman, is something the matter?" Amity called to him, breaking him out of his thoughts as her hand slid up his arm.

He turned to her and smiled, uncertain how to broach the subject of them marrying. Amity might not yet be ready for that discussion. She'd been adamant before that he *not* offer for her the night of her ruin.

He brought her hand to his lips and kissed the back of it. He had to go, take this one meeting, and he would propose later that very day when he returned. Perhaps here, but not in bed. He had to do this right.

But it occurred to him that if she was his real wife, she ought to go with him to view the Barnes estate as well. He smoothed her hair back from her face. "I was just thinking about my upcoming meeting and wondering if you would like to go riding with me to look at an estate?"

"What estate?"

"I came to the village because I suspected your cousin owned a property here, and that you might be living there. When I spoke to the villagers, I hinted I was also looking to invest. The innkeeper has arranged for me to view one estate. It belongs to Lord Barnes, but I wonder if Fairbridge means to buy it too. I'm to meet with a steward of the estate at noon. It should take a few hours all told."

"Fairbridge said nothing of buying any other property here, but then, he wouldn't normally confide in me. I haven't been on a horse since leaving London but I would love to see the estate with you."

Roman's traveling carriage was miles away and the estate was too far away to reach on foot. The fastest way to travel was on horseback. "Would you be offended if I suggested you might need to ride astride?"

She bit her lip. "No. I've done that before at Ravenswood and would prefer it on unfamiliar roads. I wore breaches belonging to Stratford under my skirts then, but I don't have a pair here."

He would have loved to see that. Amity was more adventurous than her reputation ever suggested. "I think I might have something that will come close to fitting you. I'll bring a pair of mine when I return. I'll even give you my horse to ride and hire another from the inn stables for myself if one is available."

"I can ride the hired mount," she offered.

"Only the best for you, sweetheart," he said, brushing his fingers across her cheek. "How soon can you be ready?"

"I'll need half an hour, at least."

"Excellent." He checked his pocket watch then bent down to kiss her cheek. "I'll be back before you know it."

Her expression was excited as he left the room. She was looking forward to being seen with him in public, which made his heart happy, too. He made his way downstairs, collected his hat and let himself out into the front garden. Their morning together had gone quite well so far, and he was anxious for the rest of it to follow the same fashion.

He headed to the inn and requested his horse be made ready to ride.

"I'll see to it," the innkeeper agreed with a negligent shrug of his shoulder.

The man had become immediately reserved with him upon the revelation that he was Amity's scoundrel of a husband come to fetch her back. He must have told others because there had been some disapproving looks in his direct in the tavern the evening before. He really didn't blame them. Amity hadn't described her pretend husband in glowing terms, after all.

He followed the innkeeper. "You wouldn't have a spare mount I can borrow for the day, would you? I've coin to pay for it, of course."

"There could be one," the innkeeper mused, scratching his head. "Not as fine as you're accustomed to, I'm sure."

"I can ride anything," he promised, and handed over a small pile of coin in excess of the expected charge. "I'll need both ready promptly. I promised to take my wife with me when I go to view the Barnes property."

The innkeeper sucked his teeth. "Lord Barnes will expect a pretty sum for the place."

"If my wife likes it, then it's worth considering. I'm expected there shortly, so please hurry to prepare the horses so I don't have to keep my wife waiting."

The innkeeper nodded. "I take it you've made up?"

It was a bold question for an innkeeper to ask a near stranger. But if Amity said no to marrying him, he'd be leaving, and she would stay in this village. "It's too early to tell," he warned the fellow.

He headed up to his room to change into clothing more suited for riding, making sure he appeared as prosperous as possible. Not to impress the land manager, who didn't know his real identity anyway, but to impress Amity herself.

He tossed a pair of tight breaches to give to Amity to slip on under her dress for their ride over his arm. They would be a little loose perhaps but should ensure her modesty, and if she tied a sash about her waist, it would hold them in place for the ride.

He was ready at the appointed time and went down to fetch the horses, spare breaches in hand. As the innkeeper had warned, the hired mount left a lot to be desired when compared to his own mount, Argus. But it was a sturdy beast, if too placid in temperament for an experienced gentleman rider. Amity was surely experienced on horseback, as well, and deserved the very best.

His own horse danced with impatience at his

side to be off and running the moment he was in the saddle. The hired mount merely shook his head and as Roman kicked his flanks but eventually got moving.

Amity was still inside her home when he arrived but peering out her front window in wait for him. When she saw him, it took no time for her burst out her front door in a rush of excitement at seeing him. Had she thought he'd not be coming back? Or had she missed riding as much as he suspected she might?

He dismounted the plodding hired horse and tied it to the hitching post outside her front yard. He tied up his own horse next to it, too, even though the beast kept tossing his head. "This is Argus. Energetic but he has a good nature."

"He's beautiful," she enthused, stroking the horses long nose. She glanced at him, frowning. "Is this the horse my brother wanted to buy from Tattersalls last year but was outbid on the day?"

"Hmm, it could be?" he answered, grinning that she knew about yet another revenge scheme he'd taken on her obnoxious sibling.

"I'm so glad I get to ride him instead of George. He would never have let me if he was the owner," she told him. "He'll be furious when he hears about this."

"George's temper, or lack of it, is well known now." He handed her the breaches. "For you to wear."

"Thank you." Amity darted back inside and

returned before he'd finished naming all the shrubs planted in her front garden to pass the time.

He helped her mount, though there was some confusion about getting her legs into right places on the saddle at first. She was attuned to mounting for a sidesaddle rather than astride.

Amity was laughing by the time she was secure on horseback with her feet in the stirrups. "Habits are so hard to break. I'm not accustomed to riding anything but sidesaddle now."

"Just remember to hold on with your knees and you'll be fine." Assured she was properly situated, he climbed atop his hired mount and turned toward the lane. Amity followed and they started out at a walk. "Did you have a horse of your own?"

"Not since Papa died when I was a young girl. George said I shouldn't ride alone or often, and the aunts who cared for me never dared disagree with him. If not for my cousins, Fairbridge, Nash, Jasper or Stratford. I'd never have been competent on horseback."

"Thank heavens for them." He met her gaze and grinned. "From now on, you decide our riding pace, sweet lady."

"In that case, we need to ride much faster than this plod," she warned before applying her heels and launching Argus into the lead, her laughter the only sound he heard from her until they reached their destination.

Chapter Twelve

Amity glanced around at the thoroughly neglected manor house, hoping Roman didn't actually want to buy the place from Lord Barnes. It could have been so pretty if someone had cared enough to keep it in good order some time in the past. But it would take a long time, considerable money, and dozens of staff to bring such a ruin back from the brink. And that was her opinion after seeing only the outside. She dreaded what state of decline the interior must be in.

But she dutifully played the part of Roman Crawford's wife for the sake of appearances. Allowing him to fuss with their horses, even though she was quite willing to hold them and avoid going any farther. The steward knew her from the village but spoke exclusively to her husband. It irritated her to be so overlooked for an opinion.

"As you can see, it's a grand place," the steward enthused to Roman. Pointing out features and ignoring the neglect.

The steward was either blind or delusional if he thought they were too stupid to see the faults around them. This wreck of an estate would empty Roman's coffers very smartly to bring it back to order. Although she suspected Roman could afford the purchase and bill to repair, Amity knew of dozens of unwanted estates, better kept and elsewhere, where she'd rather see him live.

The steward appeared reluctant to show the interior, too, even when Roman requested to a second time. However, at the third request, the steward sighed and wrenched open a pair of French doors with some effort.

Roman turned to her, wincing at the sound, his hand outstretched. "Sweetheart, shall we take a look?"

She'd rather not but she put her hand in his and stepped inside, nose wrinkling immediately at the dust that rose up around her. She pulled out a handkerchief to press over her mouth and nose as they toured the lower floor of the house.

Furniture had been piled up in corners without the benefit of dust cloths to even protect them from fading.

Amity could easily see why Lord and Lady Barnes wanted to sell. Only one part of the dwelling seemed livable in her opinion, and that was the cavernous servants' quarters at the very back, where the steward resided. The rest of the public rooms at the front and the bedchambers upstairs were like the outside—neglected terribly.

She went back down the stairs and stopped at

the front doors, eyeing the vines creeping around the frame with annoyance.

Roman was suddenly behind her, placing his hands lightly on her waist. "A shame, isn't it, to see a grand house fallen so far?"

"Indeed, it is," she whispered. "How could they let such a place fall so low and think anyone could want it?"

"Lord Barnes probably described the place as rustic and serene," he said, pointing to a large crack above the main doorway that showed enough light and space through to admit snow, rain, and rats. He moved away to peer into another room nearby that she knew had empty bookcases linking the walls of what should have been a large and well-lit gentleman's study or cigar room.

She frowned and followed him there. "Do you smoke, sir?"

"Never cared for it," he replied, and then glanced her way. "Why? Do you?"

"That's not done by women like me."

He shrugged. "You could if you wanted to. You are mistress of your own destiny now. There's no one to stop you doing whatever you wanted anymore."

"I thought I was a wife," she quipped. "Wouldn't my husband object?"

"He might, but not enough to consider setting her aside over such a habit."

Amity considered Roman a long moment.

They held quite a few opinions in common. They might have made a good match if he considered it. And what more perfect revenge would it have been to take her hand in marriage, too. She shook her head. He wouldn't offer for her after all this time. He just wanted to be in her bed and have fun. And it *was* fun, and she would miss him a great deal when he was gone.

"I'm having trouble coming up with a reason to fight with you. Have you thought of a provocation that would be easily believed besides the obvious?"

He frowned. "What was the obvious?"

"A flirtation with someone else."

He shook his head. "Let's not discuss parting today. Let's continue to pretend we're happily married instead."

"You know that's not possible forever."

"Why not?"

"You know why." She moved into the next room when the steward joined them, eager to engage Roman in conversation about the property.

Amity shook her head. She wasn't really Roman's wife. That made her unexpectedly angry now, and she stomped outside and back to the horses, where the air was clean and decidedly fresher than inside.

She couldn't fight with Roman over another woman—real or imagined. He'd been quite clear that he considered marriage in a very poor light. It was to be expected in a disappointed man, she supposed, but it was their only difference of opinion so far.

Marriage could be wonderful. She'd seen it. Perhaps not the way her brother had gone about it though. That union was definitely a battle neither side would ever win. But a marriage made for the right reason, for companionship and love, was certainly worth hoping for. She wouldn't mind being Mrs. Crawford, but he'd not even hinted that he might be considering her for the position.

"Amity?"

She took pains to wear a happy expression when she turned around. Roman was watching her a certain way, and her body pulsed with awareness of what that look meant. How long could she keep hiding that she wanted more from him than he might want to give? It was just a matter of time before he tired of her. But while he was here, she intended to claim his every waking moment, and his sleeping ones, too. "When did you say you were leaving?"

He drew closer. "What if I didn't go? I could buy this property."

"That wouldn't be very smart. When my cousin comes and sees you here, he would know it was you who ruined me." She looked up at the dwelling. "And it's so awfully neglected."

"It would not be if I owned it. I care for the things I love. With time, it could be a comfortable family home." He took up her hand and kissed the back. "The steward has departed but the place is not locked. Come and look around again with me."

He led her through the house one more time without saying much more about the interior, and then around the perimeter again. When he was done with his inspection, Roman helped her up onto his horse. "You know I don't ever recall seeing you on horseback in London," he murmured.

Amity controlled her horse to keep him from racing off to stay near Crawford as she answered. "Carriages only in London, so my aunts could chaperone me in luxury. Exertion was discouraged in my adult life."

"You ride very well," he told her as he mounted his tired old, hired horse.

Amity urged Argus to keep to the older beasts speed. "Fairbridge always insisted that I ride with him when I was at Ravenswood."

He glanced her way, a frown on his face. "Did you never think he might care for you?"

"Never." Amity laughed softly. "When I was younger, I both resented him for his insistence on dragging me along to ride and marveled at his intimidation of others who tried to stop him doing so. He would simply cite a long-held tradition of Sweets prowess during the hunt as his proof that I should excel at the sport, too, and drag me along."

"Using the family history against the family present. Clever."

"Manipulative," she corrected him. "Never forget that my cousin is the master of schemes within schemes. Look at how he got me here. He never told me what he intended when he took me to Lady Barnes that night after our tryst. By the afternoon the next day, I was bundled into a carriage with a handful of my own clothes taken from my chambers by a maid he must have been paid off to keep silent about it. I was sent off to the country with no idea of my heading. I didn't even know Fairbridge owned property here until I got here. The coachman was sworn to secrecy by him, too."

"I can't say I paid enough attention to his schemes before."

"You should. Hopefully it will not be too late to save yourself the eventual cost, should you ever be so unfortunate as to irk him."

"I will," he promised, tossing her a smile that warmed her insides.

If they hurried, they could make love again before the dinner hour arrived.

Amity kicked her horse forward and set off at a canter on a now familiar roadway, knowing he'd follow. Crawford let her lead, and she reveled in this unexpected freedom to still make decisions around a man.

When she reached her cottage first, she jumped from the saddle and turned to watch

Crawford's slower arrival on his hired horse a few minutes later. He came at a slow trot, a smile on his lips for her, but it was very clear to her that he was used to a more energetic animal beneath him. She openly admired his relaxed posture in the saddle, though, and that attitude seemed apparent on every other occasion, too.

Roman was a good man, and a man she should have sought out long ago…and perhaps not just to be ruined by.

If she'd met Roman before Melody had, her life might have taken a decidedly more pleasant turn. At the very least, she might even have had a friend who valued her differing opinion. He might have learned to love her despite her family. He would have been someone ready to take her to bed at the drop of a hat or shawl, too. He would have made an excellent husband for herself if he'd not been so heartbroken over another.

Frustrated at the thought of never having what she really wanted from him, she swung about for the front door of her cottage—only to find a dust-covered young man getting up from sitting on the steps.

She took a pace back, surprised at seeing a stranger she hadn't noticed lurking in front of her home.

Roman arrived and swung down from his horse and was at her side in an instant. "Who the hell are you to come sneaking around a lady's home?"

"Forgive the intrusion. Miss Sweet, I've an urgent message for you."

Roman drew back to let the messenger hand over a piece of parchment, but she noticed he did not relax at all. He hovered, eyeing the young man with suspicion.

Now that Amity's startlement had passed, she smiled at the young man. "Thank you."

He nodded. "I'll be on my way back to the inn, Miss Sweet, and will call again in the morning for your reply."

"Thank you."

When he was gone, Amity inspected the letter she held carefully.

"He called you by your real name," Roman murmured, turning to stare at her.

"Yes, I noticed that, too." The letter was sealed with black wax, but she recognized the insignia pressed into it. "This is Ravenswood's seal."

A sense of foreboding filled her, and she hurried to open it and read.

When she had, she wished she had not.

The duke was dead…and she was ordered to return to the ducal country estate by the new duke, the former Earl of Fairbridge, as his house guest, immediately. There was more but she couldn't read it because knew she could not refuse to rejoin the family to mourn with them.

She lowered her trembling hand and stared at Roman in shock. To go back meant seeing her brother again. To face the consequences of her ruin and scandal. To be talked about in the most unflattering terms and have no escape from it.

To likely never see Roman again.

He took hold of her shaking fingers. "What does it say?"

"Ravenswood is dead. I have to go back." Amity hiked up her skirts and hurried inside, beset with panic at the thought of what lay in store for her. She didn't want to go back to her family. To her brother, to her aunts' fussing. To a match with someone she could never want as much as one with Crawford now. Not now when she'd finally found contentment, if not happiness, here.

Roman followed and stopped behind her. He slid his arm lightly about her waist, his lips close enough to nuzzle her ear if he wanted to. "You don't have to do what he says. You are of age."

"How can I not go to mourn with him and my family? I'm only here because my cousin took pity on me. He could easily take away this new home of mine, my entire security, if he wanted to. He could insist I marry one of his cronies as compensation for all he's done so far."

Roman's grip tightly about her. "Did Fairbridge, Ravenswood now, threaten that in the letter?"

"I never read the whole of it. But just thinking of going back has made me feel as powerless as I was before you kissed me."

Roman pressed a long kiss to her cheek.

"According to Stratford, you are the only relative he gives a damn about. I cannot believe he would make you marry someone you didn't like after all he's done for you." He lifted her hand, and the letter she still held. "Might I read his words for myself so I can perhaps set your mind at ease?"

"Go ahead."

Amity collapsed into a chair by the fire, chilled utterly through to the bone now. It had been a glorious day, the best in her memory, until her family threatened to drag her back into the fold and crushed her spirits anew.

Then Roman suddenly cursed. And cursed again. "Damn him."

Chapter Thirteen

Roman stared sightlessly at the room. He'd thought he'd been so circumspect. How wrong he was. It was lowering to discover you'd been led on a merry dance with only one possible outcome. Especially if he wanted to live to reach an old age without holes in him.

He scowled at the neat script summoning Amity back to the family's country estate, still in shock that he'd judged the situation entirely wrong.

Amity's disappearance from London had been for one purpose alone—*to flush her seducer out into open waters so he could be reeled in.*

And like a fool, he'd never once considered he was already on the hook.

The Earl of Fairbridge, now Duke of Ravenswood, had manipulated them both.

Roman wiped a hand across his mouth, sick to his stomach over his lack of understanding. If he'd been able to forget Amity and not pursued the knowledge of her location, she might never be forced to marry him. But it was all there in the letter.

Amity, and Roman, were expected to attend the new duke's as soon as they were legally wed.

Gretna Green had been suggested—where many clandestine and expedient marriages were made. Without any annoying members of her family trying to stop proceedings. That was in the letter too. Amity's older cousin had thought of everything.

Roman raked a hand through his hair, appalled with their situation. This was not how he'd hoped to propose to Amity at all.

He glanced at her. She had her face covered and seemed in something of a panic. Amity hadn't read the whole letter yet. She'd stopped at the point where her return to the family fold had been demanded. He could pretend Fairbridge wasn't forcing his hand, but that would be a dishonest way to begin their married life.

He had no choice but to propose now, even if he had intended to anyway.

He walked up to her side and placed the letter in her lap. "You need to read it all."

"Why? It's only going to get worse, isn't it?"

"Hopefully you will not think so," he murmured, but he did not hold much hope.

He sank down in the opposite seat to watch Amity read all the words. Her eyes grew wide, her gaze shot to his several times, and then back to the letter as she continued to read. She must have read it three times before setting it down again. "Gretna? Surely he couldn't know about us."

"He does."

"But that means…"

"Indeed."

"I'm so sorry," they both said at the same time.

Roman shook his head. "This wasn't the way I wanted it to be for us."

"Nor I. You should go."

"Go?"

She looked on the verge of tears. "I never wanted you to feel honor-bound to offer for me."

He squinted at her. "What about love-bound?"

She sat up straighter in her chair. "What?"

"Surely you must have suspected I had a hidden purpose in coming to find you. I have worried for your disappearance, and, upon finally finding you, discovered a distinct reluctance to leave you again," he admitted, sliding to his knees to cross the short distance between them. He took up her hand and kissed her ice-cold fingers. "I know we hardly know each other enough yet to discuss the future, but I feel utterly bound to ensure your continued happiness. If a marriage to me will make you happy, then I agree we should wed—and it's not because your cousin suspects me, either. I have been considering ways to broach the subject since I first saw you again."

Amity stared.

He winced. "If your answer is to be no, I understand completely. I'll explain that you never wanted me when I go to visit the new duke to offer my condolences. You need not worry about my feelings in this. I suspect they are quite one-sided."

His heart thudded as Amity moved, reaching out to cup his cheek. "My husband is a scoundrel…and something of an idiot, too. Of *course* I want to be married to him. I love him. I've been waiting, dreading the day he would announce he was leaving me."

Roman's breath caught, and then relief flooded him as he took in her trembling smile. He pressed his head to hers, astonished by her words. "I'll never leave you. I love you so much more than you would ever believe possible."

"And I love you," she whispered, kissing him thoroughly. But then she pulled back to meet his gaze. "What about that estate? All those plans you were making for a future family life there."

"They were lures for you to voice an opinion on the house, and on us making our pretend marriage something real. I think I might have been too subtle." He dug his fingers in her hair, turning her face up for more kisses. "The house could be for us if you wanted to make our home here. I could be very happy living here as anywhere, really. As long as I can see your smiling face every day, I've no strong opinion on the subject."

Her fingers slipped into his hair, too. "I enjoyed talking about the house and discussing its repair, but I don't want us to live here."

"So, we're getting married?"

"Yes…yes! We are going to marry, and in Gretna Green, too," she promised, raining kisses all over his face. "And you don't need to purchase an estate for us to live in. I have a dowry, and that includes property."

He'd never asked anyone about the particulars of her dowry, but he'd always known one existed. "What kind of property? A little cottage somewhere?"

"No. Not so paltry as that. The London townhouse is mine by right of inheritance. My grandmother left it to me. George tried to contest the will because he's coveted the townhouse for years."

"Which townhouse?"

"The one I was living in when you ruined me," she told him, grinning from ear to ear. "Once it was clear he'd not get it, he obtained the late duke's approval and simply took over its management, despite my protests that I was more than capable. I will expect my husband to give him—*everyone*—their marching orders very promptly. For too long the family have had the upper hand, George pretending he owned something that was always mine. It will be my greatest delight to see my much-loved husband escort him and his wife to the door and close it in their faces."

Roman sat back laughing and slapped his

knee. "He'll think I married you to extract one last revenge on him."

Amity shrugged. "*My* revenge this time, and George deserves everything coming his way for how he's treated me."

"I couldn't agree more." Roman bowed to her. "Then I will do as my wife commands and remove the intruders as soon as I have a chance."

"The sweetest revenge imaginable must wait, unfortunately, until after the wedding. When my cousin acknowledges our marriage as legitimate, George will indeed be powerless, if he isn't already without the late duke's support. But I warn you, we will never escape them. How do you feel about Melody?"

"Who?" Roman shook his head. What a fool he'd been to pine over a woman so ill-suited to him. But then again, if he hadn't, he might never have met and had a chance to fall for Amity. And he had fallen so completely and utterly that he could barely remember what he'd once felt for her sister-in-law. He drew in a deep breath and smiled "With the old duke gone, George will be at his most dangerous."

Amity nodded. "But as you say, the new duke prefers me to all others in the family. He has already given us his blessing to marry by suggesting we detour to Gretna Green."

"So that's it then. We are husband and wife."

"Almost. There is a little matter of the formalities to be attended to."

Roman dropped the letter to the floor, widened Amity's legs and wedged himself between her parted thighs. "The first task…." He took up her hand. "My love."

"Handsome," she replied with a cheeky wink.

He laughed. "Amity Sweet, I come before you today to ask for your hand in marriage. I wish to love you and support you all the days of your life. To live and love with you for as long as we both have strength, and beyond that, too."

Tears of joy fell from her eyes. "I would be very honored to accept, sir."

Roman wiped away her tears with his thumbs and then leaned close to kiss her lips. "I'll never let you get away again."

Amity hugged him suddenly, arms tight about his neck. "I can hardly believe you will really be mine."

"Believe it." He stood, taking her up with him. He spun her in slow circles, making her laugh out loud. Slowly, he set her down on her feet. "We will leave first thing tomorrow for Gretna Green, but right now, I feel the need to share our good news with the villagers."

"You cannot tell them we're getting married. They already think we are," she warned, restraining him.

"Oh, I know that, but they're dying to hear of our reconciliation. Let's prove we're in love and never intend to be parted again. It will also give you a chance to say goodbye. We might never come this way again."

"Oh yes. I would like to say goodbye to quite a few," she enthused.

She found her shawl and went to stand before a mirror. Roman dropped to his knees behind her, put his hands up her skirts, and helped her remove the breeches of his that she still wore. He lingered there, stroking her thighs before standing up, laughing at the way her eyes shone with hunger.

"Have I mentioned how tempting you are?"

"I could stand to hear it again."

He leaned close to her ear to whisper, "I want to take you back to bed."

Her brows rose. "What about the villagers? It was your suggestion to go out again."

He groaned. "Yes. Them first, and then you're all mine."

He stood back while she fanned her flaming cheeks then fixed her hair from where it had fallen from the pins, wearing a teasing grin.

He placed her shawl about her shoulders and offered his arm. "Come along, my queen."

She laughed at that. "A tarnished queen."

"Tarnished by me, which I should never have agreed to but cannot regret now," he murmured, and then led her outside.

The horses were grazing where they'd been left, and they gathered up the reins to lead them back to the innkeeper and the stables.

Amity turned to him. "How will we leave here

if you've only the one horse?"

"I'll pay someone to alert my coachmen to our need for them tomorrow."

Amity hugged his arm. "We could dine at the inn tonight, too, if you've the coin to spare."

"A good idea." He caught her eye. "We probably shouldn't venture to your kitchen together again. I'll never look at a sturdy kitchen worktable in the same way. Who knows what we might do there again tonight?"

"No piece of furniture is safe with us around." She laughed uproariously at her own joke, and then squeezed his arm. "I'm so glad I forced myself on you."

"I am too." He looked down at her hands. "I never imagined falling in love could be so damn easy."

"Not even with…?"

He shook his head. Melody had kept him at arm's length. Amity couldn't seem to ever get close enough. She was always touching him. "It's never been like this with anyone."

As they walked slowly toward the village inn, allowing Amity to greet residents she'd befriended here, it seemed everyone approved of their reconciliation. Roman considered it luck that he'd found her, and the feeling of giddy happiness only grew when he met her gaze again and again.

Marrying Amity was the right thing to do. He'd found his forever love at last and nothing would ever separate them again.

Epilogue

Weeks later

"It's going to be fine," Roman promised Amity before he alighted from the traveling carriage, rubbing his hands together in excitement. The grin on his face was infectious, and Amity had discovered her new husband always expected things to turn out for the best. The most obvious example he quoted was the fact that ruining her had been the best thing he'd ever done. Amity had seen his point on that score. She seemed to have captured a good but wicked-in-bed man for her husband.

Fighting down trepidation she dared not allow to take hold, she inched to the doorway of their traveling carriage and put her hand in his. "Let's hope most of the family feels the same way about seeing us together."

"If they cause trouble, we will leave, I promise you that," Roman assured her. He'd proven on their non-stop journey to Scotland and back that he would always consider her feelings first. She knew he'd never allow George to raise his hand to her ever again.

She stepped out of the carriage and looked up at the vast façade of Ravenswood Palace. The Duke of Ravenswood's Sommerset home was built to intimidate. Yet there was a strange comfort in knowing that she'd been summoned here by the new duke as his special guest. "Let's hope the duke is in a good mood."

"That might be too much to ask for," Roman murmured quietly. "Let's hope he's in a fair mood instead."

"It's hardly likely given what he must be dealing with inside." She stood a moment, collecting her resolve and twitching her dark skirts about her legs. They had paused on their journey after marrying only to supply themselves with a wardrobe of mourning black, so they could honor her uncle's passing. "Now he's the duke, the aunts and uncles will be pestering him."

Roman started them toward the stairs. "What for? Money? Concessions?"

"To marry, of course. They will throw women suitable to them at him day and night." She shook her head. "Sometimes I wonder if there is a woman in the world he can like. He isn't the easiest man."

"Hmm, you might have a point there, my sweet."

Roman drew her arm through his a little tighter and led her up the stairs.

The Ravenswood butler was waiting before the door and smiled broadly at her. "Welcome back, Mrs. Crawford. Mr. Crawford, welcome. His grace has been expecting you for some time. Rooms have been prepared for your arrival for the past several days. Your luggage will be taken up directly."

Roman leaned toward the butler. "Is it widely known we are expected?"

"No, sir." The butler winked. "His grace is not known for confiding in many members of the family."

Roman exchanged a long glance with her and then grinned. "This should be fun indeed."

They entered the empty front hall to find the black of mourning had been draped everywhere. But Amity could hear the hubbub of dozens of voices somewhere not too far off. She turned to the butler. "Is all the family here?"

"Every last one." The butler nodded. "His grace will be relieved to have someone he can turn certain matters over to at last."

Amity shot a glance at Roman, who was nodding as if he knew something. "What does that mean?"

"I'm sure his grace will explain in due time."

Amity moved a bit closer to her husband. "It's been weeks since my uncle passed. At least some of them should have gone home by now."

"Barnacles and parasites waste no time attaching themselves to a new vessel and burrowing in, too. The new duke will undoubtedly need our help," he warned, patting her hand. "But let's wait and see what he has to say upon our presentation."

She gulped, grateful for his support, and followed the butler toward the rear of the property, burning with curiosity herself now. "The ducal study is this way," she whispered since Roman had never before visited the estate.

Upon entry, they found Stratford standing in the center of the room, and his three brothers there with him. Stratford seemed the only one shocked to see them together…but he slowly grinned. "You're married and not a moment too soon."

He crossed the room and embraced Amity. "Cousin, you look radiant. Congratulations on bringing the best man I know to his knees."

Then Stratford turned to Roman, and his smile utterly vanished. "My cousin! How dare you, sir."

Roman didn't respond immediately, seeming to take Stratford's measure first before speaking. "She asked me nicely."

Actually, Amity had begged to be ruined, but she didn't mind him leaving out that part of their courtship. It was somewhat romantic that after one night together, he'd been unable to forget her.

Stratford squinted—and then slapped Roman hard on the shoulder. "My God, George is going to turn up his toes or explode when he sees you two together."

"They all will," Jasper Sweet said, coming close to kiss her cheek.

Nash approached and bowed to them. "The duke has been waiting for your arrival rather impatiently."

Amity turned her attention to the new Duke of Ravenswood as he came toward them. It was no surprise to her that he seemed completely unchanged, despite wearing more jewels than she'd ever seen him wear before. When he came close enough, Amity curtsied deeply. He was the same man, but he was also a duke now, too.

Ravenswood waved her up. "Ready to face your brother?"

Amity almost toppled over in dread but with Roman by her side, holding her elbow tightly, she knew she was safer now than she'd ever been around George.

However, Ravenswood drew her away from her husband and wrapped her arm around his instead, before pulling her outside toward the hedged garden square where the family must be gathered all together, given the increasing noise.

The new duke leaned toward her. "Did you enjoy your journey?"

"Dry, for the most part."

"I meant toward matrimony," Ravenswood murmured. "Crawford was not the easiest man to divert from his singular mission, was he?"

She looked up at her cousin and detected he was fighting a grin. "No, he was not. How did you know it was him who ruined me?"

"I didn't. Not at first but don't tell him that. But, cousin. Anyone watching you, who really knew you, could surely see you favored Crawford above anyone. Of course, George got in your way, as usual."

She gaped at him. "But we'd never even spoken before that night."

"Yes, and one day I must ask you how you started the conversation that led to your ruin. Crawford's been pitting himself against your brother with such single-mindedness for the last year that I was becoming alarmed. And then he just stopped."

"So you only guessed?"

"I wasn't wrong in the end, was I," the new duke murmured. "After you left London, all the fight seemed to go out of Crawford. He had this lost and forlorn look in his eyes, and he wasn't paying any attention to other women, either."

"So, you arranged for him to discover my location."

"It seemed a sensible thing to do. If you wanted him, and he wanted you, you'd have a chance."

Amity gasped. "Cousin, I never knew you were such a romantic at heart."

Ravenswood snorted. "It has nothing to do with romance and everything to do with whose face I wish to see at my dining table. When we return to London, I should like you to act as my hostess until I marry."

"But the aunts have always—"

"I've little interest in what the old biddies want. I'm in control now, not them. Things will be different. Better."

"Yes, your grace."

"And I expect you to call me by my first name still when we are alone." He patted her hand just before they reached the opening of the hedge. "By the way, welcome to your wedding breakfast. I've had to plan this secretly myself, so none but a few trusted souls on staff actually know what the occasion is for."

He stopped in the gap in the hedge, looking over a sea of white-cloth-covered tables, an abundance of flowers, and gleaming silver table wear. To the far side was a small raised platform where musicians were standing, holding instruments. They immediately seated themselves and started to play a trill of music.

The family had been standing to one side, fiercely engaged in speaking the loudest they could to each other. Upon hearing the music, they fell silent and looked around.

When all eyes fell on Amity, she nearly collapsed from the disapproval that crossed every face turned in her direction. Ravenswood raised her hand to his lips and kissed the air above it before stepping away. Roman smoothly took his place and wrapped her arm around his again, showing off the ring on her finger.

Ravenswood moved in front of them. "Ladies and gentlemen, I am sure you will join me in welcoming Mr. and Mrs. Roman Crawford to their wedding breakfast. I'm sure, too, that you will join me in wishing the happy couple well."

"The hell I will!" George bellowed, shouldering his way through the aunts, uncles, and cousins to reach them before anyone else could.

Amity shrank inside but made herself stand tall. She'd told Roman how her brother behaved behind closed doors, and he had vowed to defend her with equal violence if necessary.

"This marriage is unlawful! I protest."

"Who else protests the match that I have arranged?" The new duke addressed the gathering as much as George. "I, for one, believe it a sound decision. Crawford can certainly afford a wife and has been a close friend of the family for many years."

"Not mine," George bellowed, shaking his fist. "He's done all he can to ruin me!"

"I recall no such thing," Ravenswood responded in a bald-faced lie. "If your investments and such have failed, it's through no fault but your own. Cease whining."

"What of her ruin?" someone yelled out from the back. That voice was Melody's, of course. Roman's first love bringing up the past unpleasantness. Amity had often wondered if her sister-in-law had enjoyed Roman's obvious suffering and acts of revenge on some level. Had she thought Roman would mourn her forever and never marry anyone at all?

She glanced at Roman, and when he nodded, she stepped up to her cousin's side and smiled at those gathered. They had once discussed how to answer this question if it was ever asked. She would lie but give an answer that was not at all so farfetched. "I wasn't truly ruined. I was secretly engaged to Roman at the time."

Being engaged made a hell of a difference to quite a few in the family.

A shocked gasp ran through the whole gathering, and George's eyes bulged. "That's a lie!"

"No, that's not possible," Melody insisted, pushing rudely through the gathering in the same fashion as her husband had done and stopping before her. Melody turned her gaze on Roman. "It's not true. It can't be."

Amity kept her attention on her brother, who she considered the most dangerous of the pair. "I said nothing then because I knew you would refuse his suit. Then I ran away to wait for him to join me. We were married in Gretna Green to avoid your unpleasantness."

Roman put his arm around her back, nodding, as the younger members of the family pushed George aside and swamped them with congratulations, particularly her female cousins, who peppered her with questions about how their secret romance was ever conducted under such close scrutiny by the aunts.

Roman remained at her side through all the blunt questioning, occasionally whispering in her ear scandalous asides that made her blush fiercely. Eventually, the aunts and uncles came over to congratulate them, a few very coolly still. But as the new duke made repeated and casual mention of the size of Roman's wealth and interest in investments, his constancy and long friendship, suspicion waned.

"I have an unentailed property your husband might find appealing, if he's keen to invest," Uncle Henry whispered to her, drawing her aside from everyone else for a moment. "Keep it to yourself though. Your brother has been trying to get me to sign it over to him for years for far less than it's worth."

Uncle Henry had no sons to inherit but a pair of spinster daughters, long past their prime, to provide for. The land was becoming too big for him to manage and selling would ensure there would be money for his daughters to inherit one day. The property also happened to share a border with the ducal estate, which made it prime real estate for the expansion one day. It was a pretty place, and Amity had always enjoyed her visits there.

"I will let him know, and perhaps we might call on you there soon," she whispered.

"I look forward to it." He congratulated her again and backed away.

Roman quickly wrapped her in his arms. "Your brother is scowling up a storm on the sidelines. No…there he goes, dragging his wife with him. Good grief, they really do seem perfectly matched in ill temper."

She turned in his arms. "How do you feel now, after seeing her again as a married man?"

"Relieved, to be honest," he promised, leaning down to rub his nose across hers. "I was never this happy before I met you properly."

She laughed. "So that's it then."

"Not so fast. There's one more matter to be discussed yet. Will the duke have put us in adjoining bedrooms, do you think?"

Loving Roman had taught her that where they loved each other hardly ever mattered. So long as she could be wicked with him, she didn't care where they found themselves. "If he expects my help, he better have put us in the same one."

Roman grinned, pulling her close enough to kiss.

Read on for an excerpt from

Desperately Seeking Seduction

Next in the Scandalous Bride's series

When Lord Stratford finds his new valet is keeping an outrageous secret, discovery could bring shame upon both himself and his brother, the new Duke of Ravenswood, whose duchy is already in dire straits. It will take an unexpected attraction, a long-forgotten painting, and a demanding houseguest to avoid a "Sweet" scandal.

DESPERATELY SEEKING SEDUCTION

Scandalous Brides Book 2

Chapter One

Stratford smirked. "It's big, isn't it?"

His companion turned obediently to look. "I've seen bigger."

"I'd like to know where," Stratford muttered, and then sat back with a grunt.

"It is impressive," Mr. Dane Winston offered with an indifferent shrug of his thin shoulders.

Stratford pursed his lips in annoyance at the faint praise for so grand a view. "Ravenswood Palace is one of the largest homes in all of England. You could get lost in there on the first day."

"I'll do my best not to," Winston murmured, a faint twist of condescension hovering on the fellow's lips. "But if I do become befuddled by my surroundings, I will ask for directions, or perhaps a map."

Stratford had been forced to hire this replacement for his usual valet, Cuthbert, who'd been injured at the first inn they'd stopped at on this journey home to Ravenswood Palace. Cuthbert couldn't have carried out his duties with a broken wing and banged up head from his tumble down the staircase, and Stratford couldn't function without a valet to clean up after him. That way led to chaos and tardiness his brother the duke would not be pleased about. Although this fellow was young, Dane Winston had been eager to escape the inn where he'd been slaving away underpaid, for a better position and wages. Even if it was only to be a temporary position.

Winston was hard to figure out and even harder to impress.

Stratford had taken him on despite only having the innkeepers word he was a sensible and dedicated worker and would give him no trouble. But as a traveling companion, Winston left a lot to be desired.

The young man's indifference to the things that mattered had begun to irk the longer they were trapped inside the slow-moving carriage. Stratford talked a lot, but Winston seemed to prefer their journey be conducted in near silence. It had already been an hour since their last real conversation. Stratford about ready to toss Winston out to ride on the back of the traveling carriage along with the groom. However, given the man's small stature, it was obvious he'd risk losing another valet at any rough spot along the way.

He regarded Winston with a critical eye, yet again wondering if he'd made a mistake plucking him out for the plum role. Stratford was the younger brother of the new Duke of Ravenswood, after all. But given that Winston had performed all the duties expected of a valet exceptionally well so far—save for conversation—he had little choice but to keep him until Cuthbert recovered and appeared at Ravenswood Palace. If only Winston had a more outgoing personality, Stratford would be entirely satisfied with his new employee.

He sighed and set his preoccupation for getting a rise out of his new employee aside until later. Coming home would be interesting. It was the first time he'd ever looked forward to it, that he could ever remember. "You can trust the butler to set you right. That man knows every nook and cranny in the place. He rose through the ranks from pot boy. As for the other servants, I could not say who you might rely upon."

Winston nodded. "I will be guided by your wisdom."

"That would be a nice change. I'm sure I told my valet to watch that step and he still blundered into a fall," Stratford complained. "Cuthbert surely must have noticed the wobble going up."

But on the trip down the next morning, he took a tumble and had broken bone. Quite an unsettling howl he'd made, too. By midday, Stratford had known he had to leave the moaning servant behind. It was not every day your beloved elder brother hosted the family for the first time since becoming the Duke of Ravenswood. Stratford was already late.

He turned to take in the view of his ancestral home. Ravenswood Palace, deep in the heart of

Sommerset, was a truly spectacular building. Four floors in total, thirty-five bedchambers. Nestled on a slight rise of land. It commanded a view of many miles in every direction.

He could not wait to see all those smug faces in the family wiped clean when they were denied the privilege of the new duke's favor. Their hands outstretched and smiles imploring, and then those same greedy hands closing over nothing but air as their smiles became a mere memory. It was their own damn fault that Ravenswood would never give any one of them a penny. They should have been kinder to him all along, rather than pandering to the late Duke of Ravenswood's whims because he preferred to foster competitiveness for his attention.

Stratford's elder brother, Algernon Sweet, sixth Duke of Ravenswood, did not suffer fools. And the family had a legion of those. He would have to be on his guard, and Stratford had counted on Cuthbert keeping his ear to the ground in the servants' hall for any potential signs of trouble and unfounded gossip about his brothers. Without Cuthbert's insights, he would have to face the family at large with more of a disadvantage than usual.

But he would make the best of a bad situation. The inn really had only the one footman who had dared apply for the position before Stratford had decided he even had need of a replacement. Mr. Dane Winston had seemed the only choice. Quite bold, too. He'd quickly gathered up Stratford's things strewn about the room, spoke with his moaning valet, and promised Stratford would not regret his hire.

And he had not, for the first days, but he would wait to pass judgement until he'd spent a few days at Ravenswood. That would surely be a test of his new valet's mettle.

When the carriage finally stopped at the front of Ravenswood Palace, he bounded out and rushed toward the massive carved old entrance doors, leaving the servants to do what they normally did when he wasn't around. It was not strictly a palace, Ravenswood, but the name had stuck, and Father of course would never have diminished the family's importance by changing it back to merely calling it an overly large manor house.

The Ravenswood butler, clad in mourning black, stepped out the doors before he could reach them, beaming a smile of welcome. "Lord Stratford. Welcome home."

Stratford handed him his hat and gloves immediately. "Good to see you, Seymour. My usual valet fell ill along the way." Stratford turned to see Winston scrambling out of the carriage. "That fellow has taken Cuthbert's place temporarily. He'll explain it all. Where is the duke and my brothers?"

Seymour nodded. "The duke is in his study,

my lord. I believe your brothers are with His Grace there, too."

"Good."

Stratford hurried inside, his boots ringing upon the marble entrance floors, and hurried toward the ducal study, keen to be reunited with his elder siblings and hear the latest ondit.

Algernon Sweet, Duke of Ravenswood, clad all in black, stood with his back to Stratford when he rushed into the room, looking out upon the lawn, but Nash and Jasper Sweet faced the door. They saw Stratford and burst to their feet.

"My apologies for being the last to arrive," he said in a rush.

"Trouble?" Jasper asked, coming closer to embrace him. Jasper was just a year older than Stratford but far wiser…and a worse rogue than them all.

"Only that my valet fell a day out of London. I had to leave him behind to recover his health and composure."

"I'll loan you mine," offered Nash, the second eldest, holding out his hand to shake.

"Not necessary. I found a replacement at the inn." Stratford ignored the hand and embraced his brother. Nash, as usual, was stiff and unyielding and their embrace was awkward and brief. He didn't know why he continued to hug his second-eldest brother. He'd simply always tried to breach his reserve, and usually failed to close the distance between them.

He turned his attention to Algernon, the eldest of them all, who had finally turned, and Stratford bowed deeply and theatrically to the new duke. "Your Grace. It is a pleasure to see you again."

Ravenswood stepped close, looking down at him with a scowl from his greater height. "You're not quite the last to arrive for the gathering," Ravenswood chided, but then ruined the complaint by suddenly scuffing up Stratford's hair, as he'd always done when Stratford was younger. He stepped back with a laugh before Stratford could attempt to retaliate. "You'll need better wits about you today," Ravenswood warned.

Stratford rushed to straighten his hair again, grinning and pleased that inheriting a lofty title of duke had not affected their bond yet. It was nice to be around family who cared about him. Algernon always had been his favorite brother, not that he wanted anyone to know that. "Who are we waiting for?"

"You'll see in due time. But first…" He gave a signal to his other brothers and as one, they closed and locked the study doors and windows, keeping everyone out. "Since you are the last brother to arrive, you are unfortunately the last to know."

Stratford stilled. "Know what?"

Ravenswood threw his arms wide, clearly agitated. "That the estate is in a bloody shambles. Not a penny to spare anywhere!"

Nash hurried to their brother's side and placed

a restraining hand on the new duke's chest before he could make a further loud outburst. "Calm yourself, Ravenswood."

"I am trying," the duke said through gritted teeth.

Stratford shook his head and looked about. Everything that he'd seen since his arrival was exactly the same as when their father had lived. "That's not possible."

"He wasted it all," Ravenswood growled softly. "Bastard left me with empty accounts and a mountain of debt plus the inevitable embarrassment of trying to pay it back."

Stratford glanced at his brothers, seeking confirmation. Neither looked shocked by the news. Though they'd probably had time to calm themselves, unlike Stratford. He struggled to believe it. They had all believed the estate would go on as it always had, just with a kinder duke at the helm. The reading of the will had not alluded to any particular problems for the estate. But the running of the Ravenswood duchy was a costly enterprise.

And now there was no money to pay for anything.

Stratford glanced at Ravenswood again and feared for his favorite brother. "What will you do?"

Ravenswood exhaled loudly, and Nash moved away from the duke. "What I must before the news breaks and the laughter starts."

Stratford's eyes rounded, and he looked to the windows and imagined the awkwardness of meeting his entire family shortly, hiding the burden of a mountain of debt. "Does anyone suspect yet? The cousins and uncles and aunts beyond us four, I mean."

"We sincerely hope they do not," Jasper murmured, clapping a hand on Stratford's shoulder.

Stratford took in his brothers' worried faces and gulped. He was the youngest, but he was one of them. A Sweet. And loyal to his elder brothers and their ambitions. "Well, I'm not going to tell anyone."

"We never imagined you would," Nash murmured, coming up on his other side. "It is vital we all pretend everything is as expected for the duration of the house party and for as long as possible beyond."

Stratford agreed. For years, they had all danced to their father's tune, waiting for this moment to arrive when they would be free. Even though they were all the duke's legitimate sons and heirs, other parts of the family had been treated far better. And to make matters worse, the late duke had encouraged that family friction and enjoyed their small squabbles. He'd had his favorites, and had always sided with them against his own grown sons. All in an effort to remain in control of their lives. To make them toe his line or risk being cast out of the will.

Those favored relations would enjoy their embarrassment when the news of the state of their financial affairs became known. Rub the loss in their noses. Ravenswood, particularly, would be placed in an awkward position. He had gained a title but an empty one.

He might be forever in debt.

Stratford had always believed that upon the duke's death, things would improve with Algernon as the head of the family. That they would all have the upper hand for once and live peacefully. But they would likely only have more trouble than before with this development.

Stratford took in his eldest brother's face and noticed the tightness of his jaw and high color upon his cheeks. Algernon was understandably humiliated by this turn of events.

Stratford gulped when Nash made an effort to check the duke's heart by grabbing his wrist to feel for the pulse. Nash would have been an excellent physician in the family if father had let him go for a proper career. As it was, he had only studied in secret, practicing his doctoring on his brothers and their willing servants. He was utterly devoted to Algernon's continued good health and happiness, wishing fervently that nothing stand in the way of their elder brother's inheritance. Nash would be watching him very closely, now he was duke. They all would be.

"What can I do?" he whispered.

Nash nodded, leaving the duke be at last. "We

have, Jasper and I, given over our entire fortunes to our eldest brother in an effort to keep the estate running smoothly, but even that is not going to be enough."

Jasper and Nash stared at him, but Ravenswood glanced away, no doubt embarrassed by their generosity. Ravenswood had always helped them. Paying off any debts incurred beyond their quarterly allowance from his own pocket so father might never know.

Stratford shuffled his feet, knowing what was being asked of him without it being said out loud. While he wanted to help his eldest brother, what he had saved himself in the last years was not very much at all. He'd never been good at keeping track of where his money went. And it seemed to have slipped through his fingers like water in recent years for one reason or another while living in London. He ought to have paid more attention to his finances.

But Algernon was his brother and the head of the family now. The man who'd essentially raised him, ensured he was well cared for all his life. Educated him, too, and Stratford had always been clothed in Algernon's finest castoffs. Father and Mother had not given a damn about their two younger sons, other than receiving regular reports that he and Jasper were still breathing. All their care and attention had gone to Algernon and Nash, the heir and spare. But that had only been to a point, as well.

He caught his elder brother's eye. "It's not much but you can have what I possess."

His other brothers exhaled. "So, it's settled. We'll sell Freemont Villa, and Highland Cottage, and now Clifford Lodge, along with those cottages you purchased from Barnes recently. That should bring in a tidy sum to keep the worst of the debtors at bay."

Stratford raked a hand through his hair and winced. Clifford Lodge had only just become his, a bequest in his late father's will. He'd spent less than a week there himself since Father's passing. He had planned to go back soon. Now he no longer could. But then again, Nash and Jasper had inherited Highland Cottage and Freemont Villa, respectively, and they were giving them up as well, so he shouldn't complain. He wasn't the only one losing out in all of this.

"Thank you, but know you won't remain empty-handed," Ravenswood murmured to him quietly. "Nash has drawn up a plan of attack and there are contracts between us to be signed. You will receive surplus profits from the ducal estate annually until the value of your sold property is reached, and for three years beyond that. You should end up richer than you are now."

"But where will I live?"

"You will stay here or at Ravenswood House in London."

"Surely you don't want me living with you," he said, laughing awkwardly. Stratford loved his older brothers, but he also knew he often annoyed them, too. He talked a lot and was somewhat forgetful. Nash was always with the duke, and he had a particularly short fuse for interruptions and conversation.

"Father may not have wanted us about, but I want my brothers near," Ravenswood promised. "You will all stay with me. I couldn't take your money any other way. You will have the advantage of having this duke's ear, for what it's worth."

Jasper caught Stratford's eye and grinned widely. "He's not that fond of us. He just doesn't want to be left to deal with the family rabble all on his own when they come banging on his door."

When Ravenswood's lips twitched, indicating unspoken agreement with Jasper's sentiment, Stratford felt a smile forming on his face, too. None of them wanted that, but it had always been easier to deal with the family together. "Our cousins and uncles and aunts are accustomed to preferential treatment."

"They are about to get a rude shock," Nash murmured. "Our new duke will soon have a reputation as a taciturn penny-pincher."

"The howls of outrage will be loud when they realize they'll have to pay their own bills," Jasper whispered. "And we will have the front-row seats to witness their many hardships."

Stratford rubbed his hands together and laughed. "This is going to be such fun."

"Don't get carried away," Nash warned. "Tread

lightly for now. You can break out into song when we have him married."

Stratford swiveled to stare at Algernon. His elder brother looked decidedly uncomfortable at the announcement of a wedding for himself. "No!"

"Yes," Ravenswood murmured. "Father has given me no choice but to marry a woman for her money. He couldn't get me to wed his choice while he was alive. In death, the bastard might get his black heart's desire."

Stratford winced. They would all be miserable if Algernon had to marry Lady Stephanie Kent, the heiress father had favored all along. A colder woman could not be found anywhere in England. She had pots of money, pride to match, and wished with every breath to become the next Duchess of Ravenswood.

So did Algernon's current mistress, Lady Barnes, although she was already married and her husband was in perfect health.

The two women hated each other.

Stratford winced again thinking of Algernon's future, caught between a wife and a mistress. There would be fireworks indeed when they returned to London.

And they would all have to answer to his duchess one day. Live together in the same house for years, too, until their loans were repaid in full. Stratford was not looking forward to that future. It would be a nightmare he'd wish on no one.

There was a tap on the door, and Jasper rushed to answer it.

But it was only the butler. "A carriage approaches, Your Grace. I believe it is the one you are waiting for."

Ravenswood smiled. "Bring her to me immediately."

Stratford winced. Dear God. Was it so bad that Ravenswood meant to announce he would marry that very day?

More Regency Romance...

Distinguished Rogues Series

Chills ~ Broken ~ Charity ~ An Accidental Affair Keepsake ~ An Improper Proposal ~ Reason to Wed ~ The Trouble with Love ~ Married by Moonlight ~ Lord of Sin ~ The Duke's Heart ~ Romancing the Earl ~ One Enchanted Christmas ~ Desire by Design ~ His Perfect Bride ~ Pleasures of the Night ~ Silver Bells ~ Seduced in Secret ~ Yours Until Dawn

Wild Randalls Series

Engaging the Enemy ~ Forsaking the Prize
Guarding the Spoils ~ Hunting the Hero

Saints and Sinners Series

The Duke and I ~ A Gentleman's Vow
An Earl of Her Own ~ The Lady Tamed

Rebel Hearts Series

The Wedding Affair ~ An Affair of Honor
The Christmas Affair ~ An Affair so Right

...and many more

About Heather Boyd

USA Today Bestselling Author Heather Boyd believes every character she creates deserves their own happily-ever-after—no matter how much trouble she puts them through. With that goal in mind, she writes steamy romances that skirt the boundaries of propriety to keep readers enthralled until the wee hours of the morning.

Heather has published over fifty regency romance novels and shorter works full of daring seductions and distinguished rogues. She lives north of Sydney, Australia, with her trio of rogues and pair of four-legged overlords.

Find out more about Heather at:
Heather-Boyd.com

Lightning Source UK Ltd.
Milton Keynes UK
UKHW010804110123
415170UK00001B/262

9 781922 733290